ALAN EDWARD

Alan Edward Roberts is the author of the novel, The Magpie, and the short story collection, A Century of Storms. He was born in Liverpool, England in 1973. A graduate of The Arts Institute at Bournemouth, and Coventry University, he currently lives in the South West of England. Cerberus is his second novel.

In praise of Cerberus

"A Greek tragedy unfolding in the shadow of the M4 in the summer of 1990. Roberts' disturbing alternative past has big themes, but his real skill is in weaving true intimacy: he's a tender poet for a forgotten generation."
Jon Woolcott

In praise of A Century of Storms

"Roberts' debut novel, The Magpie, was phenomenal - layered and intricate - and A Century of Storms shows off his talent in a new light, perhaps simpler but no less rich. The quality of writing sings and I can only hope he continues in this vein."
Richard Jones - Waterstones

"Eleven largely elegiac stories all told in a fragmented, often dream-like style leaving plenty for the more thoughtful reader to ponder. The stories are mostly melancholic and deal with the pain of nostalgia, though there are moments of absurd humour and (deliberate) abrupt tonal jolts. Shards of memory, film-like dreaminess and a love of storytelling feature prominently in this book which is an intriguing development on its predecessor."
Joe Maxwell

"Always poignant and rich in emotion."
Hannah Jury

"What I love most about this writing is Roberts' ability to transport the reader completely to a given space, with just a few deft points of reference: sound, landscape, well-rendered local dialect. Incidental characters are always more than skin-deep; everything shines and rings true."
AM Haywood

"Roberts has a thirst for knowledge and travel that shines through in his writing. He writes about landscapes that come alive in your mind and echo the thoughts of the characters. He also makes observations, sometimes tiny, that light up a scene, moving the banal to the interesting and the interesting to the extraordinary."
Trudi Clarke

"Roberts writes in a way that makes you glad to be a reader, he has laid down profound stories for us to enjoy and given us more than enough to imagine and dream far beyond the page. This author is worth getting to know, he sets a high standard in the art of storytelling."
Sandy Fish - Hartland Book Festival

ALAN EDWARD ROBERTS

CERBERUS

ROAD SONG BOOKS (UK)

Road Song Books, England, UK

Typeset in Times New Roman 10pt
Copyright © Alan Edward Roberts

Paperback edition

The moral right of Alan Edward Roberts to be identified as the creator of this book is asserted. The author of the content detailed within has the moral right to be identified as the author of this work asserted by them in accordance with the Copyright, Designs and Patent Acts of 1988.

All rights reserved. No part of this publication may be reproduced, stored in a retrieval system or transmitted in any form or by any means, electronic, mechanical, photocopying, recording or, otherwise, without the prior permission of both the copyright owner (Alan Edward Roberts) and the publisher (Road Song Books) of this book.

ISBN: 978-1-9160833-2-5

A CIP catalogue record is available from the British Library

www.roadsongbooks.com

Printed and bound in Great Britain by Clays Ltd, Elcograf S.p.A.

Mum - my life isn't the same without you

Flossie, my darling dog, this book's for you girl

Also by the author

Fiction
The Magpie

Short stories
A Century of Storms

"There's something very powerful about being absent."
from Steven Soderbergh's 1995 film, The Underneath

"I once had a dog and his name was Spot. I once had a dog and his name was Spot. I once had a dog and his name was Spot..."
from Jane Campion's 1990 film, An Angel At My Table

1 | Cerberus

1975

The Chorus | Some far-off command...

I recall the creature from my waking dream – it was clearly rendered, this heavy-set Alsatian as it stood close to the centre of a frozen lake encircled by conifer trees. It was barking and I could see the miniature clouds of its breath, yet I could not hear its call. I was experiencing a bracing coldness and was shivering as I waited on the shore. After a time, I began to feel the presence of more dogs.

First of all, I saw their exhalations plume – inverse silhouettes cast against the blackness of the forest's understorey. Then, as if obeying some far-off command or design, the crowds of sheltering animals broke the cover of pine trees to engulf the surface of the lake en masse. My perspective then changed – seen from high above, I watched the lake's icy skin as it became obscured by the rivers of dogs. Their amassing bodies transformed the silvery white expanse into a seethe of brown, black, beige, ochre, orange, and golden fur; a wonderful swirling calligraphy of canine beasts

– it was as if something unseen was conducting them from inside the shadows.

A wild algorithm of Dachshunds, corgis, Jack Russells, beagles, lurchers, Alsatians, St Bernards, Chinese crested dogs, mongrels, poodles, cocker spaniels, Rottweilers, Dobermans, pitbull terriers, blue heelers, golden retrievers, Dalmatians, foxhounds, Portuguese podengoes, Chihuahuas, Canadian Eskimo dogs, Pomeranians, collies, Labradors. More dogs. These magnificent beasts of earth and rock, woodland valley and field.

A cascade of paws. My utterance of these words caused me to jolt myself clear of sleep's undertow. The quiet had been rewired from an absence of sound into one which now housed my voice. Beams of early sunlight divined along the bedroom walls through the morning window, and I listened for noises to understand from the other rooms in my apartment – on the wireless, a woman's distant voice communing like a ghost trapped in my walls, and then outside, the birdsong – a collection of garrulous blackbirds – a car swishing along the wet street below. A new day – the same set of reasons to move – I'd overslept. The ever-reliable Maggie, her day mapped out to the minute, her habits defined in an invisible ledger for organised good dogs, hadn't yet come to nudge my foot with her cold nose the same way she always did - get up, get up it's time for breakfast! An inquisitive sniff, a lick of the face – where is my Maggie? Where are you my beautiful girl?

Summer 1990

Luca | Changes and days...

On sunny days like this, I'll more than likely walk out into the crops with a library book and a beach blanket. Maybe I'll take a couple of cold beers from the restaurant along with me – sometimes I do, sometimes I don't. I'll then find a crop hollow to unwind in – just lie down, work the kinks out my backbone, either read or simply close my eyes and listen to the field move.

If I'm feeling particularly untroubled, I'll stay hidden in the field until the evening or until about half an hour before my shift begins.

Right now, I'm thinking about new recipes to try out on my brothers, Andrea and Roberto – they're getting harder and harder to impress these days but at least I know I'll have some firm ideas for the specials board if, by some act of divine providence, we ever make that a 'thing' again. They are good guinea pigs most of the time; Andrea loves his seafood, and Roberto is keen on spicy veggie dishes. Mamma on the other hand would drown everything with cheese if I wasn't there to stop her. When she is tableside, when it comes to Parmesan cheese on the customers' food, she begins to scrape and scrape and never stops until they are begging for mercy. So many good pasta dishes, like my spaghetti alla Norma, and cacio e pepe, ruined, but it's just local families that come inside Carmine's, they like what they like – always the same few big sellers off the menu. I mean, if you have the local monopoly like we do, then good or bad who cares? All we've done is focus on the presence of a local appetite, no more and no less, and I am convinced most people will pretty much eat baked beans if we were selling them. Indian, Chinese, French, Italian, no matter who occupies the sole restaurant unit in Eton Wick, the locals would lap it up. They don't care; I'm not belittling our customers when I say these things, they're really nice, mainly, but they're pretty unadventurous, and we reflect that by what we provide for them. Anyway, it's chicken and egg, isn't it? I am always battling with Mamma to tell her that we can do so much better for everybody. I want them all to love my food because it's amazing and because I care, and not just because our restaurant is the only one in the village. My late grandfather, Don Carmine, would weep if he could taste some of the things I've had to rush out on a Friday or Saturday night, but if the customers don't know their Ricciarelli dolce from their tinned ravioli it's not my fault or maybe it is, it's like somebody punching you in the face again and again with your own fist – I send myself crazy thinking about it, yet Mamma will not budge. The people who come through the door, I've known all my life, they are nice people; why not do something special for them? Show them something new from our region of Italy, I

5 | Cerberus

want to do a free taster menu evening for our most loyal bunch of regulars, but no, Mamma says our family don't have money to throw around like Michael Jackson. She has no vision, no scope for daydreams – she says we are winning so why lose in the spirit of creative enterprise – it's too risky. Anyway, Mamma and Roberto continue to write down precisely what the customers ask for and the world continues to turn, but I suppose sometimes boredom can be instructive and because of this, the specials board will most probably always be an old people's home for spiders.

This week it's been very crazy, but then there's always some kind of high drama going on at Carmine's. Roberto is not speaking to Andrea because last Sunday when we were preparing the kitchen, he found a pair of lady's knickers in one of the giant sauce pots. He had left the Arrabiata sauce to marinate in the walk-in fridge overnight, went to stir it and found the renegade undergarment, sopping with the thick red sauce. Roberto went off like an atom bomb, kicked a hole in the office wall, then he threw the entire bucket of sauce all over Andrea's Ford Sierra. There was a big brawl in the street which took about four people to break up; it was like a scene from West Side Story. I don't think a single serious blow was landed during the whole scrap though – Roberto had a bruised cheek, that's all. He is the smaller of the two but way faster than Andrea and uses the flat of his hand to slap rather than punch you. Andrea is built like a heavyweight boxer but is getting soft around the middle, meaning he's very strong but easy to tire and slow-moving too like the boxer George Foreman was during his prime years. Do you remember? Muhammad Ali used to call him The Mummy. As a result of the fight, Andrea has been banned from coming into the kitchen after closing time – five times this has happened in the last year or so. Always, after a night down the pub, or after he's been to a club like Henry's or Valbonne's, he'll let himself into the kitchen, break into the fridge, cook something, then leave a gigantic mess behind him, tipping semolina everywhere as he sets out to make a pizza. He wrecks the dough and ruins the yeast Roberto and I have been saving for weeks. Most of the time Andrea's pulled some girl and taken her back to the kitchen for a bit of fun and he'll always try to impress them by whipping up something tasty to eat, except he can't cook for shit. God knows what he does with these women on the work surfaces as well; he's got no shame, but honestly, he can get in where a draft couldn't – I've seen him with all kinds of women, some very beautiful ones too. Maybe it's his broken nose – it never set properly after he got hit in the face with a crash helmet years ago – somehow it makes him look more distinguished, some may say charming. Anyway, how am I supposed to know what these women see in my older brother? There are more questions than answers, that's for sure. Because of Andrea's behaviour, Roberto, me, and our pot washer, Ashton, had to clean the whole kitchen again before we could begin the prep work for the afternoon-shift – an extra hour or so was needed just in case we got randomly inspected by the Health and Safety goons. I instructed Ashton to help Roberto to make a new batch of sauce because I didn't have time to do it; he'll be a good chef one day.

Every time, it's always the same, after a few weeks of good behaviour, Andrea comes back and then we have to fight him again, get Mamma involved. This is the main reason he just cuts hair now, wherever the restaurant is involved, he's like this great big hungry racoon – a busy pest. But Andrea is Mamma's favourite and he'll worm his way back in just like he has every other time. If anybody else messed with the running of the restaurant the way my eldest brother did, they would end up in a biroldo, it doesn't matter who – delivery men, staff, fridge suppliers, bank managers, everybody, you just do not mess about with Carmine's or Mamma will put you in some serious caca.

I escape here to the fields to tune out all that noise: Mamma, my brothers, Helen and her husband; their antics all fade out to nothing when I'm here.

If I strain my ears, I can hear the girls I just cycled past talking and laughing, but apart from that I can't hear anything out of the ordinary beyond the far-off cars on the M4, a motorbike in the distance somewhere to my left, insects chirping, the sailing of crop heads. I often watch the stems dancing and speculate that they are communicating with me via semaphore.

As I lie here, I am focusing on the sky that happens on forever. There's more than enough blue to make a sailor's shirt up there, and I feel good.

Hope | I was too slow…

It was a case of first come first served at work, but I was too slow to ask for time off to go to Luca's funeral.

Gene, Casey, Astrid, and Rowan all beat me to it. So, it was me and the manager, Ash, who got left to run the shop whilst the others all got time off to pay their final respects. I tried to explain to Ash that the others didn't even know Luca as well as I did – that I knew him from Carmine's as my family always go there. Ash just told me it wasn't his place to judge who could and who couldn't go to the funeral; first come, first served was the fairest way and if I could persuade one of the others to swap with me then he didn't care either way. He asked me who Luca was and then he didn't even stick around to listen when I began to fill him in. He does that a lot, asks you how your weekend was or something and then walks off without waiting to hear what you have to say.

Anyway, I followed him through the shop as I described my friend Luca to Ash as being this cool guy who was way older than us. That he was head chef at Carmine's over in Eton Wick, and it took all his time up; that he didn't have time for a wife or a girlfriend or anybody really – just his family at the restaurant. Everybody thought Luca was really handsome and that some of the girls I go to school with well fancied him. I told him everybody in Eton Wick loved Luca's food and we all went to Carmine's for birthdays and other special occasions; that he would bake these incredible birthday cakes, and his mum and brother, Roberto, would make a real fuss over us every time we went there. Andrea, his oldest brother, has a men's hairdressing salon called Rossi Brothers next door to the restaurant; he is funny and is always singing along to his Louis Prima and Claudio Villa tapes, talking Italian on the telephone, placing bets at the bookies. Andrea always pours a glass of red wine for his best customers too; I think he's probably one of Eton Wick's biggest characters.

As for Luca, he would always say hello to everyone, riding around town on his bike with a bag full of groceries swinging off the handle; he doesn't mind sharing his cigarettes or buying a bottle of Strongbow from Mr Varma's for us as a few of us are still underage. Luca would swear us to silence. I own the cops, he'd joke. I'm even cool with the judge. Boodlal and that said Luca had got those words from this horror film he'd seen ages ago called Once Upon a Time in New York.

Ash just nodded when I'd finished telling him about Luca but he surprised me when he told me he knew him; that they were in the same year at school. He was a real smoothie back then too and they all called him Luca the Looker or Pukka Lukka.

Ash is all about the job and he treats us like slaves – the last manager, Parminder, she was way nicer but she moved over the motorway bridge to the eastbound shop a few months ago.

Astrid | Out in the fields...

Me and Casey went to Luca's funeral together. We had to request the day off from our jobs at Eton Wick Services, Ash was good about letting most of us attend.

We were told Luca's body was found out in the fields where he always goes for a lie down whenever the sun's out. We were sat on the Stairway to Heaven that day and remember him cycling past without his shirt on. Imogen wolf-whistled at him and he blew her a kiss, laughing.

I can't believe we'll never see him again. He was so nice. I can't stop thinking about him.

Hope | Genuinely there...

I'm livid. Rowan and Gene didn't even go to Luca's funeral after booking the day off work. That is bang out of order. They went record and clothes shopping up in the West End instead and they blatantly used Luca's funeral as an excuse for a day trip together. When I complained to Ash, he said it didn't matter to him what people did with their time off, he reckoned it wasn't any of his business. I cannot believe I didn't get to pay my respects to my friend, and I had to do three times as much work to cover for that lot. I don't mind covering for Casey and Astrid, they were genuinely there. But the other two, well if they want a favour off me, they can get go and get stuffed, I'm through with them.

I took ten quid out of the till as damages, but from a different day's banking, when I wasn't working, Ash owes me big time. He didn't even say thank you for all the extra work I did or bother to get relief in from the eastbound side.

Rowan | A soundless dialect...

I let Mum braid my hair yesterday whilst we watched A Room with a View on video for the eight hundredth time. She says it's cinema's greatest advert for true love. Each time we see it we find ourselves perched at the edge of our seats waiting for that poppy field scene where Julian Sands takes Helena Bonham Carter into his arms and kisses her passionately in the tall grass – it gets us every single time. Kiri Te Kanawa on the soundtrack doesn't help matters either – I feel my heart swell every time. I bought the soundtrack when I found it in Oxfam last year; I'd play it constantly on my Walkman whenever I was painting at college. Nobody knows I like opera; Gene would shit a brick if he knew. He thinks it's for lemons.

Sitting watching the film with Mum is just about the only time I see her in escape mode. Most of the time, I don't even notice she is at home; it's as if she has discovered the mysteries of silence, crossing between rooms as if she is walking on feathers, sidestepping the nightingale floor seemingly able to avoid each creaky floorboard, pouring her Portuguese coffee without a single sound. She only smiles in her sleep; I watch her closed eyes and wonder where she goes but whenever I ask, she claims she doesn't dream.

I'm not sure why Mum stopped running her salon. She just closed it all up one day about ten years ago, it probably had something to do with the dogs. Our kitchen still has a beauty counter set up, with this outsized barber's chair in the corner of the room, stacked high with old beauty magazines – it's too big for the space; there's a sink and mirror, lightbulbs around the edge like you'd see in a theatre dressing room. I get her to do my hair every now and again to cheer her up and it works, kind of. Tonight, we sat at the kitchen table to choose some beads together, and once we'd decided on a set (we'd picked some green and yellow ones out) she patiently threaded them into my hair – it took us both ages to find any floss in the cupboard though, we nearly had to abandon the task. Now it's all finished, I think it looks lovely. I wasn't allowed braids at school until I was in fifth form, but since doing my art foundation course at college, I've left my hair loose because the novelty of wearing them had worn off.

Friends have been encouraging me to apply for university recently but it's too late now for this year. I'd have to go back into college to take photographs of this really big spray paint portrait I did for my non-existent higher education portfolio, but I can't be bothered and now the campus buildings are all closed up for the summer. It's currently hung in one of the hallways over there as each year my old college chooses a tiny selection of final pieces for exhibition before they all get filed into the county archive. I did a portrait of Mum and Dad called The Reality.

My dad, Ysrael, moved out when I was a baby. I think he lives in the north of Portugal somewhere, he sends Mum sporadic cheques, that's it. At the head of the staircase, there's a framed photograph of him in his old army uniform, he has a neat moustache and tight curly hair beneath his beret. His mouth is slightly ajar to display a neat row of sharp looking teeth – his dark eyes are sleepy and big and almost uncannily circular; he reminds me of an angry cartoon mouse. That photo has been the sole representative of his whole life. It's the one I used as the basis for my painting. Mum never talks about him directly, I've gleaned about six sentences from her about him, that's the sum total. She told me once the only thing men do well is walk away, that they take their intentions and promises with them leaving only shit behind. Am I shit?, I thought when she said this, then I realized these words were meant for somebody quite separate from me. She could have been talking to anybody. I did the painting to provoke her, but she has continued to keep him all to herself, I think she still loves him because she'll pick his photo up to dust it whilst the rest of the house is just left to wrack and ruin. There are no other traces of him at home except for me.

After Mum finished my hair, she looked at our reflections in the mirror with what I read as a sense of pride then she retrieved a creased photo from under a fridge magnet – every time I see it, I'm bowled over by the over-saturated reds, greens, yellows, whites all vying for power. In the shot, Mum is aged about nineteen, her own hair braided too; it was taken back when she was growing up in Porto. She is stood under the awning of a carmine-coloured city square bodega, the sun hitting the rows of bright soft-drink bottles, chocolate bars and magazines, yet in the distance you can make out the shapes of people and the blur of a large humpbacked car, pink blossom. She was wearing a white and black hooped t-shirt and drawing on a cigarette, her left eye slightly obscured by a smudge of smoke. I think my mum was most probably comfortable with whoever was photographing her – maybe the person who snapped her was in love with her and had already taken about three reels already that same day – she had that semi-bored, confident look about her. It was as if she knew the camera just as well as whoever was behind the lens. It's a much better photo than the one of Ysrael, but no more relatable; I feel locked out of both.

As we stood looking at the picture together, she said we could have been twins but even at her young fresh age she still looked far away and beyond my reach. We don't look alike.

The Chorus | Never leave us…

It says somewhere that three-quarters of people live within twenty miles of where they were born, and I'm no different. All your landmarks and monuments are right there in your face, the places, even those which have been demolished. You can't help but notice the way you've been captured and reflected by your surroundings. You can never keep these things out; they are you and vice-versa – you are them.

Years ago, there was this red diesel silo at the edge of the beech woodlands and farm fields out on Common Road; it's long gone but its tall concrete staircase is still there – like a shortcut into the skies. The kids today call it the Stairway to Heaven and they mainly hang about there and smoke cigarettes, play music, skateboard, set fireworks off – it's a place to go – it was for us too once the silo, the farm workers and their buildings had all disappeared. The ones who go there these days don't even know what the stairs were used for, maybe they asked around once but the answers they were given weren't worth holding onto.

After thirty years and change, I'm leaving tomorrow. I'm

hopeful I'll return one day but it might not be in the same state as when I left it – in the end we lose our hand hold on everything, but I really want to try and keep everything with me for as long as I can. As I walk through these spaces, I am imagining I am the human embodiment of a tape recorder, or a film camera; my concentration is optimised so I'll be able to replay these moments when I'm living far away. I'm imbibing the light, the sounds, the feel, the detail.

The fields unburdened themselves of a scattering of rib bones of a long dead dog that had been unearthed by the last big rainstorm; it's been fifteen years since they all went extinct. I know with certainty that the remains are that of a dog because their distinctive bones are commonplace in the British countryside. Instead of the sanctioned mass pyres offered up by local councils, people unanimously took to the edges of their towns and villages and held unofficial funerals for their lost pets. Whilst many chose to bury their dogs in their gardens, others chose to inter them in farmland, woodlands, beaches, and their local parks. Nobody really mentions the dogs anymore, everything has already been said. It's like we can't believe it's happened to us, even now.

I've now stopped to observe the gathering clouds shaped from vast coils of the earth's rising hot air, I notice the ensuing blackness of the sky contrasted against the departing orange, pink, teal expanses of daylight. I pick up the shrill calls of the wheeling starlings, trying to fix my eye on them as they go; instead, my vision gets caught on a pair of bats as they rapidly spiral towards a border oak.

Do you ever hear that bassy thrum that sometimes comes at

sundown? It sounds like a million dogs growling at the back of their throats or some colossal granite monolith moving to seal a doorway in a mountainside closed. I can feel the bass in my gut, all through my bones and organs, and I am too scared to move until it stops. Again and again, I find myself intimidated by this unnamed majesty in nature and I'll feel the need to halt, hold my breath, and listen.

Astrid | Blue-black feathers...

On my way back home from work today, I found a sleeping crow on the path. I was halfway across the farm fields near where Luca died, between the motorway services and the village, when I saw it. At first, I thought it was dead. I stopped to watch it, but I didn't know what to do – I almost walked past it and left it there, but something made me take a closer look. I had my Halina Paulette in my bag with me, so I took a few shots of it from different angles – I only had five exposures left on the reel. I saved the last shot for a closeup of its oily looking blue-black feathers with my macro lens; that's when I noticed its breast moving up and down, but its eyes remained closed.

I crouched down to pick a dried-out twig up off the ground and I poked the sleeping bird very gently with it to awaken it, but it stayed the same.

Gene, who'd left work a bit after me, had caught up to me on the path and asked me what I was doing. I don't like being alone with Gene because he's scummy and probably wants to go out with me even though he's with Rowan. He smells of cheese and onion crisps, Lynx spray, and weed all the time. He's mostly negative and has a mean answer for everything.

Gene stopped and looked at the bird for a second then the idiot went and kicked dust at it. I didn't like him standing over me – I told him to leave the bird alone and to stop being such a git.

Ignoring me, Gene told me he thought the bird might be dead; I had to point out to him that it was asleep. Then he took a jumper out of his bag and rolled it up and placed the sleeping crow carefully on top. This was surprising because he never has any good ideas; he went on to say we should show it to one of the old people in the pub, that they'd know what to do. It's the only sensible idea he's ever had around me.

On the way to The Shepherd's Hut, I asked him why he didn't go to Luca's funeral, and I mentioned that Hope had really wanted to go. He said she should've just called in sick and left Ash to cope by himself if she really wanted to go that badly - that he'd have been able to find cover from the eastbound shop.

When we got to the pub, we took the bird inside and showed it to this boss-eyed woman behind the bar, but she told us to clear off before screeching all over the place about vermin. Anyway, one of my neighbours, Old George, was sat at a table with another fella in the garden and waved us over. He explained he wasn't supposed to be there as he was still recovering from an operation and was essentially off the beer, which I thought was a stupid thing to be boasting about. We showed him the crow which he informed us was, in fact, a rook.

Old George suggested getting the pub cat to sniff at it, so we went and grabbed Polly and let her have a bit of a nose at it. We placed the bird down on the ground and suddenly, the bird woke up and jumped to its feet, hopped once or twice on the spot and flew up to the pub roof. Polly wailed a few times at the rook which had positioned itself on the lintel above the front door. We stood watching for a minute or two but before long Old George and his mate headed inside to buy more drinks. Gene offered to buy me a drink, but he's gross so I carried on home and wondered what it was all about. When I got in Mum was doing jumping jacks to Electric Avenue by Eddy Grant. I could hear it all down our street. She loves that song.

Gene | The note inside…

Luca's family closed the restaurant down and the family have moved back to Italy, that barber brother of his too. I guess they couldn't face being here. The note inside the window said they planned to reopen Carmine's after the summer but loads of people are saying they won't be back.

I didn't see Astrid much outside of work after the day we found the sleeping bird. Her boyfriend, Lance, began picking her up at the end of our shifts. He has this souped-up Ford Fiesta with fat tyres, a spoiler, a massive aerial for CB radio, and one of those 'On a Mission' stickers inside his back window just like every other shit fast car around here does. He's this real fucking 'Kev' who listens to all that Under-5s Top 40 bath toy dance music through his big speakers in the boot with no treble in the balance. (((BASS))) Woo…Yeah!/Woo…Yeah!/Woo…Yeah! Probably loves Kylie and Jason too, and all that other Stock Aitken and Waterman bollocks.

Hope, at work, is spreading shit around something rotten about me and Rowan because of Luca's funeral. Janet Street-Porter hoe, she literally won't do a single thing for me, won't even so much as hold a door open, or come to the till when there's a queue. I complained to Ash, and he said real Gs don't grass. What a cock.

Rowan went and apologised to Hope, but I don't get what the problem is. We'd been planning to go to London for ages. She's just stirring it. All the lads call her Nutty Snacks because we always see her sat in corners reading poncey novels and eating Tracker bars and Bombay mix, picking stuff out of her big hippo teeth. Neil Patterson said she touched his 'hairy banana' (his words) at Valbonne's. Neil is constantly lying about all kinds of things certain girls have done to him when most of them wouldn't go anywhere near him even if he was made of Tampax. Neil recently got expelled from college and lost his weekend job because he was caught by the cops helping to roll an unattended police car into a ditch at a warehouse party raid. Now that is a true story, but he won't talk about it, oh no! Fucking blabbermouth – whenever he's telling one of his porkies, we sing a bit of Big Mouth Strikes Again by The Smiths at him to piss him off but he still does it; he's like the guy in You Talk Too Much by Run DMC. Every time I see him, he tells me Mike Allen's show is coming back on Capital Radio which is patent bullshit. Anyway, we mostly listen to Tim Westwood since Mike Allen stopped doing his show 3 years ago, well, I do anyway. Most of the others like Pete Tong, Jeff Young, Steve Walsh, and the pirates in West London like Friends FM.

We have our own local pirate station I hang out at called Red Shoes FM that broadcasts out of different blocks of flats in Langley. It keeps on moving around to avoid detection by the DTI who have been hounding us ever since we got picked up by air traffic control at Heathrow – the red eye from New York was trying to land and it picked up 110BPMs of dope noise instead.

A mate I've known since first school, Manjit, has a show with his older brother Mukhtar on Red Shoes FM and whenever we buy any records we go over to the studio and he'll spin them on air, and maybe we get to say a few words into the microphone. His show is called The M Brothers House Party, and he plays all sorts just as long as you can dance wicked to it. Manjit tends to play a lot of Hip Hop, as well as loads of Rare Groove, House, Jungle, Balearic Beats, Electro, Swing Beat, and Hardcore-hybrid stuff, all kinds. My mate Bob Funkhouse does mixes live on the show; he also DJs at The Old Trout. Bob and the M Brothers are all in this group called Slough Boys & Indians (S B *& I): Mukhtar calls himself Big Justice, and he's the producer, there's Ashton the Raggamuffin Monster who's the MC, and then there's this oddball called Johnny Double-Glazing who wears the thickest glasses I've ever fucking seen who's like this special dancer like Bez from the Happy Mondays; he just shows up whenever we play live and we've kind of adopted him – we don't know anything about him really. S B & I, pretty much makes bleep music, with sped-up beats nicked off old records layered with echoey reggae-style vocals. We were all in the studio a few weeks ago speeding up and looping the breakbeat from Isaac Hayes' Joy for a track they wanted to make – Bob found a copy in the RSPCA shop on Wexham Road and took it straight to Mukhtar; it's gonna be ill. I used to lend them my Ultimate Breaks & Beats LPs for samples, but never my hip hop imports because they always mash-up my good vinyl – they fucked my import copy of To The Max by Stezo and I can't find another one to replace it with anywhere, just the UK pressing which is on shitty thin wax – you can make Rolf Harris wobble-board noises with it. As S B & I, they've managed to make one record so far; it's called Dubmarine and they play it on their show all the time, but it's a total rinser man, trust me. This woman from Horsemoor Green Youth Club helped them find rehearsal space and showed them where to apply for small grants for time in recording studios – Duke of Edinburgh's and that. Mukhtar and Manjit's dad, Deep, runs an Indian women's fashion shop in Langley called Mumtaz where you can buy saris and dresses and shit. He wants Mukhtar to work there but he's always too busy with his music and his dodgy business deals, he's also got a full-time job at a tyre shop on the Bath Road where he began as a YTS dude. He's just spent a bunch of money on a car and music kit for the band too. On the other hand, Manjit works for his dad, and then he makes most of his scratch by selling small amounts of puff and sniff out the back door of the shop. He's always getting in trouble with his dad for going to sleep on top of the boxes of clothes, leaving the front of the shop unattended.

I do my level-best to make tapes of the M Brothers Show whenever it's on, and years from now I can maybe sell them for a lot of money to people who live in the past. I did that old jingle which goes, now hear this! Free Mandela! Free Mumia! Free James Brown! RIP Yusef Hawkins! DJ Scott La Rock RIP! Bleeeeeeep Apartheid! To my brothers in South Africa, stay strong. Rock On my mellow. Red Shoes FM ya rule. And this other one that simply goes, Red Shoes FM presenting live and direct on all channels. Real rudeboys and bad girls turn the dial to the M Brothers Militant Mayhem Show, seen? That's my copy of King of the Beats by

Mantronix playing in the background during announcements. I need to get it back off them before they ruin it, or it gets smashed up or confiscated in a DTI raid.

Hope | All narrow...

when a *[handwritten: haves для U name, there'll be.]*

There is this new guy starting at Eton Wick Services with us because Astrid is leaving to go to university next month. His name is Brian Palmer and he's a friend of Astrid's boyfriend, Lance. He's got a funny bowl cut and a really red face, and very straight white teeth. I think he's got a face like a super villain in a cartoon – all narrow eyes and a big, weird chin like Roger Ramjet. And his eyes are very blue, and he could be good looking if he wasn't a beetroot, in fact that's what everybody calls him, Beetroot.

I met him at this house party about a month ago, and he had this little notebook where he was writing down girls' names inside; the ones he wanted to get off with.

Beetroot is one of the Car Freaks who drive up to Winter Hill just to talk to each other on their CB radios all night even though they're all parked up together in a row like morons. Beetroot likes necking pills and he might even deal a bit, in the autumn he sells fireworks too – he talks like he's big time. I don't even know why Ash gave him the job as he just looks like a trouble-turd. He is going to be part-time including most weekends and mainly doing evenings so we will be on a lot of the same shifts together. My school has ended now, so I asked Ash for more work, he said no, not until he'd worked out who was stealing from him, as the till was short ten quid most days. It's not me, I only take money when Ash pisses me off.

Beetroot starts next week; Astrid said he'd probably be at another free party Lance was helping to arrange at some barn out Dorney way. If I go, I am going to have to creep out the house because it's an all-nighter. It's funny but the more I think about it, the more I want my name to go in Beetroot's book, but I don't want to snog him, I don't like his hands. They look red raw; I don't think I want him to touch me. He's ratty.

Astrid told me Beetroot's notebook of girls is called Schrodinger's List after this supposedly famous experiment with a dead cat in a box. I don't get it. If you're on the list, are you a dead cat?

Rowan | The belly of the whale

I have decided I'm going to finish with Gene soon. I never see him and when I do, I wish I was somewhere else. He is out most nights, hanging out with those radio bods from Langley. Besides, him making me go to London instead of Luca's funeral made me feel so bad afterwards. And I had to really apologise, I mean, you know, beg to Hope for her to forgive me – but I was genuinely sorry, and I still feel like shit. She's about to do the same art foundation course at college that I've just finished, and we have a lot in common, so I'm bummed I've wound her up. I know I didn't have to go, but he'd been promising to take me to London for ages and in a stupid trance I just went along with it all. It was completely crap anyway, all we did was traipse around crowded record shops, and we had no money for lunch because he made me lend him all my money for this record he badly wanted - then we argued all the way back on the train. It was the absolute pits. We never got to go to Carnaby Street or Brixton or Camden Market – we just moped around Soho. I swear we were on the same street all day. The only good thing I saw were the mosaics by Eduardo

Paolozzi down in the London Underground station on Tottenham Court Road but to be honest, that doesn't add up to all that much because I didn't get to stop and have a proper look.

All I got to eat in the end were some Spangles I found in my bag. I wanted to buy a T-shirt from the Soul II Soul shop and a belt from Four Star General but I hadn't taken anywhere near enough money up with me. I'll have to go back when I get paid and not with Gene. Hope was alright in the end but Gene still won't say sorry to her, and he keeps on referring to her as Nutty Snacks which is plain ugly behaviour. Hope is so beautiful in this really unique way, and Gene isn't a kid anymore calling people stupid names for kicks. He seriously needs to make amends; Luca was Hope's friend, and he was always alright to us. When I think of my own behaviour, I feel queasy; I pinch my arm until the feeling of wretchedness goes away.

Once or twice this summer, I followed Luca out into the fields as he really intrigued me; he never knew I was there, or at least he never let on that he did. I saw him out there on one occasion with this older woman called Helen who runs the bakery on the main road. They were talking for a while, and laughing, then they dragged each other's clothes off and had sex. I was so embarrassed, it happened so quickly, but I couldn't move from my hiding place as they would have heard me moving or seen me, so I stayed hidden.

Helen already has a boyfriend or is married; she mentioned a man called Rude Ron a few times, how she'd had to borrow his car to get to the bakery – this big old Mercedes I've seen around which has stained yellow headlights like cars in France.

Anyway, this Helen was having a great old time. Afterwards they just lay naked next to one another talking and joking. I heard her tell him that her life could be boiled down, quite simply, to the killing of time between the instances when someone said the words, 'I love you' to her. She said it like this: life is just me killing time waiting for someone to tell me they love me. I don't care whether they mean it or not, and it can be anybody. I just get an electric charge from it… Then Luca kissed her for a long time, and then said, Helen, I love you. This made them burst into laughter, and she slapped his face as a joke. It's never been like that between me and Gene. It's been three months since we started going out; we never lie around together laughing. There's no comfort, after we've been together, I feel like I always leave with less than I had before. There's no ease. He's not kind enough. He calls girls hoes and skeezers, and he smacks me on the bum in front of his mates, and then they think they can all do it too. When we were in London, Gene bought a record with a song on it called Mr Big Dick which is about his limit really. There's nothing there anymore and I think he's a pig. It took me seeing Luca and Helen together in the field for it to click that we're doing it wrong, that I'm doing it wrong. We're way off.

There is a free party out in the fields soon and I'll probably dump Gene then. I think the easiest way to go about it is just by kissing someone else and making sure he gets to hear about it. If he gives me shit at work, I'll just leave and get a job at Daniels in Windsor or ask Parminder if I can work on the eastbound side with her guys.

Hope bought me a burger and chips from the Wimpy up at the

services after I said sorry. She invited Astrid too and she told us all about Luca's funeral, how it was very sad and how his mum broke down crying. How his brothers, Andrea and Roberto, both set a pair of doves flying from their hands at the end of the ceremony, and that one of them flew back inside the church and sat on the crucified Jesus carving's head. Andrea and the priest tried to coax it back down, but it flew about and poo'd on the altar. The send-off of the doves was beautiful though, she said. In the service, they played Con te partirò (I identified it when Hope hummed a bit of it for us – she has a nice voice). Then Roberto read a section from one of his favourite books, Pinocchio; it was the part where the puppet finds Geppetto in the belly of the whale.

Astrid said an announcement was made at the pub after the funeral where there was a function being held for all the mourners. The family said the restaurant and the barbers were going to be closed for the summer. That they wanted to mourn in private and come back to Eton Wick in the autumn. Nobody got drunk at the pub. At some stage of the afternoon, Andrea had come over to talk to Astrid and Lance and she said he was very upset and felt helpless in case his brother was in danger and needed his help in the afterlife, that he hated thinking of Luca out there, lost without his big brother to help him. How can I help him now? He is dead and I am alive, he could be in trouble, he'd said. Then, Astrid told me, he cried and hugged Lance close to his chest for a long time. That Helen woman was at the funeral too, with the old ladies from her bakery; she left a yellow rose on his coffin.

The next day Ash had us all in the office after close to say that somebody was stealing and he'd already reported it to HQ and that from then on, he would be setting traps to catch the thief. What kind of traps? I asked him if he was going to put a mouse trap in the safe but on and on he went, telling us that in parts of Mongolia they chop the hands off of thieves and feed the fingers to their children or parents at a ceremonial barbecue.

As he laboured on, Ash told us from that day onwards, he was to be the only one who could go inside the safe – the keys would never leave his belt or that of a trusted day captain's. He looked at Casey when he said this – did he think she was the robber or that she was to be his new right hander? We all knew the thief was Hope anyway, well me and Astrid did, not sure if Casey knew, probably not; and Gene was clueless and could well have been stealing too. In fact, with the exception of Astrid, we'd probably all had a dib in the till at some point. I rarely do it, I mainly take food. Money's too easy to spot when it goes missing, no one gives a fuck about a chocolate bar or the odd bag of Quavers. Casey steals cigarettes: it's what Hope told me anyway.

Astrid | His Alpines...

Casey asked me and Lance to give her a lift home over to Chalvey as it's sort of on the way to Lance's flat, so we did. Her car had broken down and she was late to get her kid from her parents' place as they had tickets to go to a meat raffle at The Flags. I had to squash in the back because Casey couldn't fit; it's very cramped in there because Lance modified the boot to make room for his Alpines. He played music all the way to Casey's parents', and it was hell. I don't mind his music, but you can't hear anything except for the drums and the low end when you are sat in the back. He put a tape on, so he didn't have to listen to Casey talk about how hard her life is.

Years back Casey got pregnant by this random seventeen-year-old Australian virgin. By the time she found out she was with child, he'd disappeared off down under again. She had none of his particulars except for his first name and that he lived in Brisbane!

Eventhough she had no hope of tracking him down, she decided to go full-term and keep the baby – she confessed that she was afraid of abortions. This was three years ago now, maybe four and ever since her son, Huey-Mitchell, was born she's been on a mission to save up enough money for a trip to Australia in order to find the kid's dad. I'm trying to imagine what it would be like, her showing up at your front door saying congrats you're a father! And this is your son! Say hi. It may never come to pass but she's going to give it a shot anyway, at least she'll get a cool holiday out of it all. I've heard that Australia's lovely.

I've heard her tell this story about ten times so far and little details change so I don't really know how much to believe. What I do know is that Casey's been saving like hell for the day she hits ten grand, then she's off on her trip. She reckons another year and a bit and she and Huey-Mitchell will be off to find the mystery dad, unless she goes and gets pregnant again.

Everybody thinks Casey wants to get with Ash. They are always off having smiley conversations with each other, and she blushes whenever he says nice things to her when they think they are in private, but we all see them. Casey's the only one Ash is kind to or has his lunch break with; they act really cute as they eagerly team up for tasks at the drop of a hat - he stacks the high shelves, she does the low ones, little things like that. He brought her in some sweets his mum made for the Mela in Upton Park earlier this year, and she made him some chocolate brownies back as a thank you. Retch.

Rowan | Together most days…

At work, Ash was telling us all about when he used to be in a band called Monsoon in the eighties; he told us he played guitar and had long hair, that they'd had visions of being an Asian Def Leppard or Whitesnake or something. They even got signed to a label and released a single called Marry My Sister – it got to something like five hundred in the charts. I don't believe Ash has ever done anything remotely interesting with his life. He'd brought his record in with him and some photographs to show us he was cool once. I still think he's a knob though; having long hair and playing guitars isn't even 'in' these days. We just all went, yeah cool. Then rolled our eyes at him behind his back and cringed. He's just a clueless plonker and I'm sure some of his stories are just a bunch of 'Billy yeah man' anyway.

I know Ash is with Casey though. They have lunch together most days and he treats her better than the rest of us put together. They are quietly laughing all the time, canoodling in the storeroom - sometimes he gives her a lift home. I can picture their fat jelly bellies spilling everywhere when they're doing it, his splodgy red-nosed face frozen in ecstasy. They're well suited – both of them are annoying and repetitive. Casey's probably just stringing him along until she can go to Australia to find Huey-Mitchell's daddy. I think her little boy is kind of cool though. She has a photo of him Sellotaped onto the front of her locker and he looks cute but pretty chunky for a tot. He reminds me of a tiny version of Hulk Hogan mixed with that Aussie tennis player, Pat Cash, with his wet-look hair.

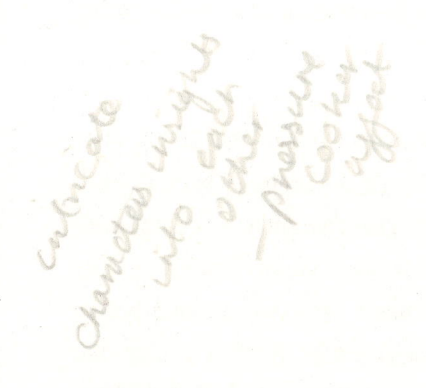

Astrid | Like golden grass heads…

We were all out at Winter Hill to watch the sunset. Eight Car Freak vans showed up that night, so I took a few Polaroids and some reportage shots with my Halina Paulette of their vehicles all lined up in a neat row with the guys all posing about – most of them are pretty used to me bobbing about with my cameras so they ignored me most of the time after the novelty wore off. I'm hoping that a fair few of the pics will come out looking nice and natural. The light in the sky made the edges of their hair look like golden grass heads.

Beetroot had fitted some new speakers onto the inside panels of his Fiat van. Whenever speakers need a workout, the guys always play this bassy track I love called Let's Get Brutal by Nitro Deluxe which Lance says is the Car Freak's national anthem. It got played so loud the vibrations made a side panel fall off Beetroot's van. He was not happy. Things were made worse when Lance began teasing Beetroot about Schrodinger's List. He was getting hot under the collar, and all the girls cornered him to see if he'd added their names inside. But he just got in his van and drove off in a huff.

I find Beetroot and his book totally creepy; I've said as much to the others. For ages, I thought the list was just in his head until I saw he had an actual notebook. If I ever get my hands on it, I'm going to put a match to it. I asked Lance why he had to tell Beetroot about the vacancy in our shop and he just shrugged. Now there'll be three sleazes at work.

After Beetroot disappeared down the hill, everybody went back to their own vans. Lance smoked a J and we just held hands and watched the sun go down. It seemed to take an age for it to vanish behind the horizon, but I didn't mind.

Gene | Before the summer ends...

I've never seen a dog, I'm not old enough to remember our family dog, Drum. It was something called a Westie; we have a few photographs of her in the living room and in albums. I'm told Drum doted on me when I was a toddler. Dad has often said dogs were always a lot more relatable than cats, more comfortable in our presence and that they could express their devotion to us with little effort. I don't recall Drum at all, I have no replays in my head, but I've seen lots of dogs in films like Digby, Plague Dogs, and The Incredible Journey, so I know how a dog moved and sounded but I get no sense of my own family's pet. I feel like my dad's generation are haunted by them, and I really can't tune into how they're feeling unless I go to this place I know called The Pit.

The Pit is this secret spot we go to where this local graff artist called Slave does these massive life-paintings of dogs - ten-foot-tall murals. There's this Alsatian piece under the M4 where the train tracks run beneath it; it's only about fifty yards away from the hidden entrance into The Pit. I think Slave must be older than us if he can remember dogs in that kind of detail.

41 | Cerberus

I want to find out who Slave is because his art is so amazing, I wonder what his connection to dogs is. I'll talk to Bob or Manjit, maybe we can stake the tunnel out or The Pit itself before the summer ends and see if he turns up.

The Chorus | Nothing stays…

I remember hearing Cattle Call on the radio on the afternoon Sailor and so many other dogs died. It's almost as if Eddy Arnold had spirited him away with his otherworldly yodeling. Do you remember the song I'm talking about? That song comes to mind whenever I think of that time. It's this kind of song that asks me to cry every time I hear it, then comforts me until I stop.

When I travel back to those days, I recall the details not the sentiments; it affected us all in very different ways. Every time I play Cattle Call, I begin to weep. I can't help it. I think of my Sailor. I can't see it any other way than this, I've had something stolen from me, we all have, us old dog owners. And no-one will or can help me find what was thieved all those years ago.

Nothing stays the same. All things come to pass they say, and yet, we don't manage to hold on to anything by the end. Nothing remains and nobody and nothing can break this spell. The dogs… they're all gone.

Gene | All I see...

At Rowan's house, their living room is decorated with this wallpaper with thousands of dogs on and it goes all the way up the stairs too. All different breeds, it's been there for years. Her mum, Antonia, is doggy gaga, she goes to this thing called Crufts every year where everybody celebrates the lives of dogs; it's this big televised event buried on some weird satellite TV channel which Dad has, so I've seen it out of a morbid curiosity. The oddballs who go there all take these giant framed and mounted photographs of their pets up to the NEC in Birmingham and walk around with them in circles on big green mats. The event reminds me of church or something because there are guest speakers from all these religious groups, then everybody sits and watches hours of old beauty pageants and horse jumping displays for dogs on these colossal screens. There are stores where people sell rare dog pelts, and there are surrogate dog people who dress up as pets and you can cuddle them, lie down or roll around with them – they wear scents and pheromones to evoke all the senses of being around a dog. Others sit around plaiting old dog hair you can buy by the ounce. I've even seen in very rare cases that taxidermized dogs are displayed and sometimes sold. There's doggy mediums who hold seances for gullible prats that want to contact their dogs in the beyond too. It's a real self-pity fest, with everybody crying because dogs have gone extinct.

I'm told if I'd lived at the same time as dogs, I would feel the same way, but I didn't. All I see is sad people. Rowan's mum's living room is full of photos of her old dogs, and the various trophies her dog, Trudy, won at different shows before she died. The whole ground floor is basically this shrine to them. She reckons the government should have intervened; if it was humans facing extinction they wouldn't have hesitated to help. I don't believe that though.

Rowan | His flat kiss…

I have an interview next week at Daniels Department Store, then I will talk to Gene about giving him the flick. He doesn't even try to do it with me anymore, not that I want him to, we've given up I think, and it's just dying on its feet. I feel myself physically recoil whenever I bring him to mind, every time when I think of him touching me, and his hard, unsubtle fingers, dark rings around his eyes, his flat kiss, his lazy red dick like a sweaty sea creature.

I don't know how he got in. I don't even remember, it's almost as if he just showed up one day and stayed – all the air he's sucked out of everything, and it has made me forget why I liked him in the first place. Disappointment seems to be his endgame – it doesn't trouble him that he can't create or inspire anything good. Without any lightness, you can get so easily discouraged from everything. Your sensibilities all conk out.

Last time I saw Gene, he was telling me his friend, the weed seller Manjit, is in hospital because he has fallen into a coma of some kind. Like one day, his dad found him asleep in the storeroom at Mumtaz and couldn't get him to wake up. I'm supposed to go up to Wexham Hospital with him, but we have to get two buses to get out there. I don't even know Manjit properly plus he's the one who slapped my arse just because Gene did.

Mum kept me awake with her crying last night. All throughout she cried calling for Trudy and her other dogs.

In my bedroom, as a kid, I had illustrated dog wallpaper same as in our hall and the living room, but I redecorated when I was old enough to know what I was doing. By the time I was of primary school age, I'd scratched out every single dog's eyes with my fingernails because I didn't like being watched through the dark – I was terrified of them. I used to fear the darkness really badly, never used to be able to go anywhere without flicking a light on first, but maybe all children hate the night. But over time you learn not to mind the things that scare you out of necessity because you discover there are way worse things to be frightened of especially when they are seen in daylight.

Hope | People can pigeonhole us...

I've made myself late for three shifts on the trot whilst applying my mascara and lipstick before work, but nobody's said anything about how I looked except Ash who told me I looked like Beetlejuice. I completely hate him, he looks like Morph off Take Hart. I've been totally skint ever since he's been setting traps in the tills – I've had to settle for taking food instead. I told the new guy, Beetroot, that he better not 'teef' any cash out of the till because it's been booby trapped. He didn't believe me but said he didn't have to steal anyway because he's a baller. Judging by his coat he's full of shit - it's PVC leather and reeks of hot fish - you can smell it a mile off. Saying that though, I don't actually mind him all that much, and he really has been pitching in at work. I think Ash likes him already.

I asked Beetroot about Schrodinger's List, and he pulled a face and called Lance a dickhead for talking shit. I wonder if he's added me to his book. If I sort of put my hands on him here and there, just lightly, he might ask me out and I can do something obscene to him in the back of his van one day. I really want him to see what

I'm like outside of work so he can see how I dress, my long boots, my full-length real leather coat, and stuff, then he might get the idea that I'm a pretty cool person when I want to be – I should just tell him to come down The Fawn, save me from all the second-guessing and mucking about.

Wearing a work uniform is deadly if you love clothes, how can you know anything about anybody when we only get to look like a bunch of sorry Fruit Pastilles? It's a quiet exercise in turning us into slaves, attempting to make us behave like dumb servants and I also think it gives people a license to treat us like dicks when they're the dicks. It all just serves to lazily put us in our lanes where people can pigeonhole us. Retail equals loser to them, they say it's unskilled, which is not true, it's honest work, better than having to sign on or do some non-job generating a false economy – social climb all you like, we don't need people like you/them.

Earlier this week, me and Beetroot were talking on the benches outside at lunch – he was telling me about this super bong he'd been building. I ended up showing him some ideas in my art book that I've got for a tattoo I want on my back of this creature from Greek mythology called Cerberus. Cerberus, in case you don't already know, is this giant dog with three heads which guards the exit to Hades – he stops the damned from escaping back up out of the underworld… I want to get good at sketching animals, so I've completed dozens of pictures of animals' bodies and their anatomy – joints, bones, heads, legs, torsos, muscles, veins, sinew, skin, fur, teeth, claws. Anyway, all my talk of the underworld inspired Beetroot to tell me about the time when his younger brother Michael, who used to be a hardcore glue sniffer, saw a demon in the multi-storey car park down Victoria Street in Windsor. He'd said it was green and had peeled itself off the bottom of a car before disappearing inside a puddle of engine oil.

Rowan | Laugh this way…

I don't think young people should be allowed to look in mirrors – nothing good comes from it. I don't agree with the way I look or believe this is the face everybody I know sees.

I used to sketch my face all the time, chasing my image down with charcoal but I don't get all that much from my self-portraits anymore.

This isn't how I imagine myself when I go about my day-to-day stuff; I think I look different to the girl looking back out at me – prettier, better defined, steelier. At least it explains the way people treat me. That person looking back out at me is the very same person Gene once asked out, tried to impress with his own sketches, blocky soulless paintings, and endless Hip Hop compilation tapes. Maybe this is the real reason why I can't bear to hold my own gaze. If Gene likes me, then what does that really say about me?

Astrid | Lasts for days...

Those idiots Gene and Beetroot have become best friends just because they both like the same kind of music. All they talk about is Red Shoes FM, rap music, car sound systems, smoking weed, bongs, crisps, spray can art, skateboards, fireworks, action films, football, and DJing. Or they just spend hours doing Spitting Image impressions of idiots like Roy Hattersley and Douglas Hurd, however this week it's been a barrage of repeated lines from that new film, Total Recall, and shit Arnold Schwarzenegger impressions - consider that a divorce, zzzz. At least they aren't being perverts anymore, but they barely do any work either, I mean how long can you stand around talking about Flavor Flav or Eazy E? Somehow, they can do it for days on end. I told Lance, but he wasn't at all sympathetic, he just said the name of the game in jobs like mine is to get the most money for doing the least work, so when they stop working I'm supposed to stop too. He also told me Beetroot had started stealing boxes of energy drinks whenever he was on the late shift alone to sell at free parties – I can't stand him and I intend to warn him off doing that, and then if he persists,

I'll say to Ash. I don't care if I get called a grass. I honestly cannot wait to start my degree in London then I can leave that place – leave these duffers behind.

Lance, Beetroot and some of the other Car Freaks are going to Ibiza to get caned for ten days in a row. I'm not into getting pilled-up, supposedly the comedown is murder and lasts for days - Lance double-drops and all sorts and takes all kind of prescription drugs that they all steal from their parents and swap around between themselves. He told me he wasn't worried if I didn't want to take anything - it was my choice. He explained there are two kinds of people: those who can take ten pills a night every night without getting affected, and then there's the other kind of person who can take a half an 'e' once, just once, and then lose their minds forever. And that if I thought I was the latter or I didn't want to find out which one I was, then not to try, to just have a drink instead. He told me he'd still respect me - it wasn't about being a chicken or anything; we could still have it large whenever we liked, which made me laugh – it sounded so naff even though his sentiments were welcome.

Some people wonder why I'm with Lance, they say he's beneath me, but he's not. He's decent. He's worked hard to get where he is. He's had nobody to show him right from wrong, and he's made it. He's twenty-one and he's already got his own place, a good job, a car, and he's got a future. I don't care that I'm moving away because I love him. There is beauty in other people, he's the proof.

Gene | Cut the head off the snake…

When Rowan ditched me, she was very brief. She didn't mince her words. She came straight out with it. I'd met her after work (she was off that day) at the Stairway to Heaven and right away I knew something was off. She was stood with her arms folded waiting, and she was looking at the jogger's watch I'd bought her from Argos for her birthday as she spoke. Her reason for chucking me was that she thought I was sexist and selfish and she hadn't felt right ever since we went to London and missed Luca's funeral. She said the whole day had made her feel like shit and my refusal to acknowledge how wrong it all was had pissed her off even more and she couldn't hack it anymore.

I hadn't seen any of this coming at all because she's the same all the bloody time. Just surly, and borderline miserable every time we hang out together. She also told me she'd found a new job at Daniels so we wouldn't have to see each other at all after tonight. I asked her if there was another lad on the scene and she just scoffed at me and said I'd put her off going near anyone else for an ice age. I believed her, but I'm gutted all the same, I've got to say.

Rowan has been my only girlfriend and I can't believe it's fizzled out just like that. She asked me if I had anything else to say, as she wanted to cut the head off the snake there and then. Imogen Slater had told her that binning someone had to be done quickly like tearing off a plaster – a slow death will only lead to hate and crying. Personally, I think she hates me already. Rowan climbed to the top step like she was trying to get away from me. From where she chose to sit, all I could see was the glare of the sun which was setting quickly by then; I had to shield my eyes to outflank the light, I couldn't make her out properly unless I moved. She asked me if I was crying. I told her I wasn't, but I was reeling.

Rowan told me that that was that and I asked her if she needed me to walk her back home, and she said no thank you and that she was sticking around to meet Imogen and some others, then she pulled a book out of her handbag and started to find her page. She dismissed me, just like that. I mustered up the word, bitch. And then pegged a clod of mud in her direction before walking off. I heard her shout 'fuck you' at my back and saw the same clod skim across in front of me and break up on the road. I wanted to tell her I loved her instead; I don't know why I threw mud at her but I did.

After I'd pulled myself together, I decided to call around Bob's house, but his mum said he'd gone to The Trout to set his decks up for the night. I'd lost track of the days, Bob always DJs there on a Thursday night. I went home, heated up some red cabbage and potatoes for my dinner, then got on my BMX and sped over to Windsor to see him. I took along my spare copy of Eric B & Rakim's Seven Minutes of Madness record with me that Bob had already given me money for. A tidy two-pound profit for a couple of pints.

When I got to The Trout, I told Bob about Rowan and he just bought me a beer and dedicated his next record to my plight, Dub Be Good To Me by Beats International - conversation over. He knows I have a soft spot for the original by The SOS Band but the remake is dope even though it's a pop tune. Whilst that was doing its work on the crowd, he encouraged me to select a few records from his crates and after a few swallows of John Smith's I was alright again. I saw a few people I knew; Boodlal came over to the booth to tell me Manjit still hadn't woken up, but it wasn't a coma, he was simply asleep. He told us he was in the room at the hospital when Deep (his dad) had tried to shake him awake but the nurses had intervened.

Despite the double downer of Manjit and Rowan, Bob managed to cheer me up. He admitted that he'd always thought Rowan was a major misery guts, and I joked that shagging her was about as exciting as ten year's worth of the Queen's speech and all she ever did was lie on her back and close her eyes until it was all over. How she never made any noise, or kissed me back, that her hands were always icy, her kneecaps were weirdly furry, and she smelt like wet clay. Bob just nodded ironically and said, that sounds fun, before he went back to working the crowd. Who wants to talk about girlfriends in the DJ booth anyway? No one.

We ended our set that night with Three Dog Night's Joy to the World. Bollocks to the world, bollocks to the boys and girls, bollocks to the fishes in the deep blue fucking sea, and bollocks to you and me.

Astrid | Slipstreaming other cars...

There was a big fight at ours last night. Mum's boyfriend, Crap Craig, tried to kiss my older sister, Synnøve, who was visiting from London. He tried to kiss her when they were both sat at the piano. She'd been practising the adagio of Bach's BWV 974 and said he just leaned in and kissed her on the cheek whilst running a hand up her leg. Of course, he denied it, and Mum started having a go at Synnøve at first asking what she'd been doing to lead him on, then she threw Craig out when he called Synnøve a cock tease and a fucking liar.

Even though she backed her up in the end, I couldn't believe Mum didn't fully support Synnøve over Craig's violation, and this caused uproar. Mum said stuff that suspiciously sounded as if she was trying to excuse him which was pathetic. He touched her and went in for a kiss, how can that be anything else but what it actually is?

I don't even know where Mum picked Craig up from. He's awful. At twenty-five, he's much younger than she is. He has a company car, this sleek white Benz 190E and he snorts coke like a hoover – he's always sniffing. Craig likes to brag about driving at top speed down the M4, slipstreaming other cars, flashing his headlights, until they get out of his way. He told me he loves the feeling of seeing the streaking lights of the other vehicles all around and it makes him think he's in a cool pop video – he thinks he's being this introspective poetic type but he's all surface, stinking up the place with his Paco Rabanne cologne. Synnøve told me that he styles himself on James Spader out of Pretty in Pink, only he's not very good at it. His blonde hairs get everywhere too, we're always finding them. I think he moults more than a horse.

Last weekend, Synnøve took me to a club called The Limelight up in London, she knows the doorman, Winston, who is friendly with a lot of people on her dance degree course; I didn't have to show my passport to prove my age or anything. We danced all night to something called Rare Groove which was all trumpety and funky. It sounded old but the crowd really liked it, some people were even breakdancing which I didn't even know people did anymore. Synnøve bought me drinks but told me her friends might offer me drugs in the loo by asking if I 'partied' or if I was 'sorted' – I know all the expressions already because of Lance's friends but I suppose as she's my older sister she felt the need to point things out. The crowd in The Limelight was very mixed with straights, gays, whites, West Germans, white dreads, blacks, Asians, soul boys and girls, Americans, Aussies, post-punk revellers, and Japanese tourists – a real cultural melting pot all coming together to party. I had a really good time and after the club wound down, we walked back to Synnøve's over Waterloo Bridge as the sun was coming up. We could hear people giggling as we crossed the span; one of the dancers said the bridge was probably made from marijuana (then we all started laughing because she pronounced marijuana with a hard 'J'). Another dancer that I'd been chatting to for most of the night called Enos tried to kiss me; he put his arm around my shoulders and with his free hand lifted my chin to meet his lips, but I pulled back and told him I had a boyfriend. It was very smoothly done, but then, he is a dancer – so stealthy. I wasn't angry or anything, he was really cool about it and didn't push his luck. I was kind of in awe at his efficiency - Synnøve told me that in her degree they all study body movement and connectivity no end – so beware of dancers, love's black widow spiders. Enos was very quick to set his error aside as he seamlessly went on to tell me he had begun rehearsals for a piece he'd devised with a friend instead. It was to be performed in the autumn at some festival or other at Sadler's Wells. He suggested I ask my sister to see if we'd both like to go and watch him on my next visit to the capital, either way I was invited and he'd get me a free ticket. I interrupted and let him know I'd be living in London myself by then after I started doing my degree in September. I didn't mean all that much by it, but I think he read something into my reply that wasn't meant to be there, but I think it's so difficult to tell what's me and what's other people. Anyway, for the rest of the time we were all together, he kept a physical distance and we just chatted within the group or little spin-offs of our own here and there. He's nice looking, I think he looks a bit like that Crystal Palace footballer Ian Wright. Enos has a shaved head though, and is, I'd say, about five foot eleven – he says his surname is so long and unpronounceable for most white people that he just introduces himself as Enos N. I told him nobody knows how to pronounce Synnøve's name when they see it written down and she doesn't call herself S; then I told him he should give people more credit. He laughed at this and said I had a good point. He then showed me his name on his university ID card and I have to admit, it would take some serious concentration to spell it correctly let alone say it right without help. It is Nwachukfu.

Around sunrise, all the dancers arrived at this massive warehouse flat in East Dulwich. In the centre of the floor there were about six mattresses covered with heaps of blankets and throws. Everybody just piled on and passed out. It was fun. I was tired for days afterwards.

Crap Craig doesn't live with us; he lives in Windsor somewhere by the Safari Park. He has invited us all over for tea with his parents a load of times, but it feels weird. I think he's a sleaze but in a different way from other perverts I've had the misfortune to encounter; there's a confusing need for violence in him that I can't put my finger on. Also, I really don't like the way he watches me all the time, and I know he's looking whenever I get up to walk around, I can feel his gaze on my arse. Mum doesn't see this stuff. She'll be besotted with him until the day she isn't anymore; she'll just drop him when it suits her like she did the last guy, Ricky. Ricky was nice though, he respected us, and pretty much stayed away from me, you know he let me have my privacy, and he was good to Mum and vice versa. She just got fed up with him being around ours all the time in the end and he was always skint because he had a gambling habit – the slots. He used to cook these impressive spreads about twice a week; he worked night shifts at the Mars factory and used to bring us chocolate bars all the time too - Twix, Star Bars, Topics, loads. Now we're stuck with Craig who won't even so much as wash a cup or peel a potato.

Synnøve told Craig to leave her alone and stood up from the piano and shouted for Mum. Mum said Synnøve was no longer a child, and he was just being nice which is unbelievable and makes no kind of sense to either of us. After the row Craig just went off leaving us to pick up the pieces. Heard his car roar off up the road. He'll be back though, sadly. He'd left his Filofax behind so when Synnøve and I went down The Greyhound for a drink to let Mum cool off, we threw it into a ditch. Typical guy, she said, starts shit and then storms off somewhere. Synnøve was incredulous that Mum didn't back her up as well. She told me she thought Mum was jealous of her and Craig which is ridiculous. Synnøve can have her pick of guys, she's so sophisticated.

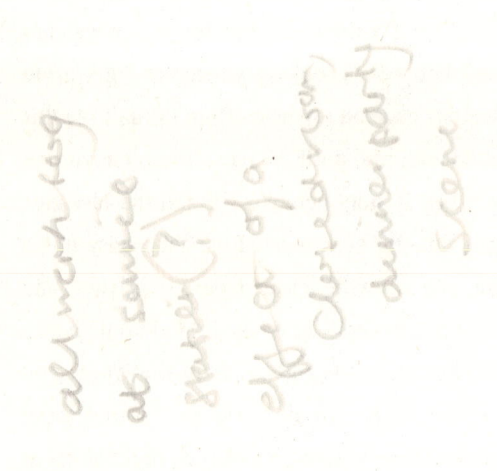

Hope | They want to sleepwalk...

Yesterday, I went to the care home to do some sketches of the 'inmates', as Mum calls them. Mum was working but most of the time I'm welcome to come and go as I please; she's a carer and she says although most old people are lovely, a few of them can be arseholes. Mum definitely has her favourites, but she says the worst of the inmates are often men - those who have been made weak with old age and increased infirmity. Men who had once had good jobs and lots of people working under them, strong men who could no longer even go to the toilet by themselves. I get it totally; they were once powerful and now they need to have help with everything. But some of them are mean, and callous and that makes their carers the same. Mum doesn't take any crap, but she says she'll treat everybody with dignity no matter how they treat her, and as far as I can see, she does. Many of them are under strong medication, and their behaviour is not always their fault, some of them have dementia and you can't afford to take what they say or do personally, they are very lost and very ill. Being compassionate is the most important and complex part of her job, and that's the bit she's best at.

I regularly makes sketches of this lady who lives at the care home called Joanne; she told me once that she had been an amanuensis for a famous writer who used to live in Dorney right up until she retired. She'd lived at the author's house in an annexe and when he died, and the estate was sold, she found out he had left her his home in his will. Joanne never had any children and doesn't have any living relatives; I wonder what happens to people's houses when there is nobody to give them to. I told Astrid about being an amanuensis because she wants to be a writer, it could be good experience. When we were talking about it, I couldn't remember the name of the job, so I told her Joanne used to be a salamander.

I was a bit put out the other week when I showed one of my tattoo sketches of Cerberus to some friends at school, they all brushed me off and started to go on about Nicola Martin's new baby instead. She is seventeen like me and she has just given birth to a little girl she's named Morgana. They all go on like it's something amazing, that a baby is a victory for love but they're a bunch of boring morons. Almost any woman can get pregnant, it's hardly unique. I mean, there's a ton of babies born all around the world every second of the day, literally, and yet we all go on about the miracle of birth and fawn over each other's infants like they're something special. If babies are so outstanding where do all the zillions of ordinary nobodies come from, all the bores like Ash, the straights – where do the weirdos, murderers, bullies, druggies, cheats, and the hordes of wankers we encounter everyday come from? I mean by comparison, I drew a few pictures, and they're the only ones of their kind in the world, they are unique one-offs yet there they all are squawking on about how cute their identikit babies are – it's so phoney. I'm going to be like Joanne, I don't need to have a bunch of selfish kids to make my mark on this world. I don't need to join their dumb one-size-fits-all club. Rather than standing out, I think they exist just to become a member of the majority – well I guess that's their choice if they want to sleepwalk. I don't want kids – my womb is a boarded-up room and it will stay that way.

Joanne's employer used to write these acclaimed novellas, I bought a few from Hammicks last year; the most famous one (I'm told) is called Final Approach. It's the one where each of the elements begin to misbehave, like ice didn't melt it caught fire, fire dripped like water, each element's entropy was completely muddled up. And then there's this woman who could choose her sex, gender, age and appearance at will like a sci-fi version of Virginia Woolf's Orlando I suppose. It packed a lot in and was pretty good except it didn't stick the landing – it just stopped in mid-air. I guess I'm used to reading books where the endings are tied up and no loose ends are left dangling, it's The Italian Job of literature. I lent my copy of Final Approach to Boodlal and when I got it back off him, he'd used the back cover to make roaches with. He waved me off and went on to say he didn't need books to read, that he was enrolled at the University of Bob Marley. He's such a cliché, he's all about dusty records, spliffs and stinking up the place with his crusty feet every single day. I haven't had time to read any of this author's other books yet, although they are all really thin. They're not cheap either. I think I might have even stolen one from Hammicks to make up for how expensive they are.

I wish we could barter for stuff in shops depending on how many were sold around the world at a given point in time, like the stock markets. Shopping would be way more interesting and involving if things like that happened.

Anyway, all those girls who were talking about Nicola's fat baby were causing this massive queue for the toilets and I was bursting. I really bloody hate it that boys can just go and have a pee and come straight back out without hanging around. I want to know why, when they build these places like schools and offices, why the men's toilets and women's toilets are always the same size, I mean there are more urinals in the boys, so more boys can go. Us girls take longer to go as well, I read that we retain less water, so we pee more than males, and also, we have to tend to our periods, and personal hygiene a bit more, so why are they all designed to be the same size? When I asked Mum, she said it was the same at work, tiny women's staff loos for them and a pristine unused loo for men, of which there are none at her care home. It's because most architects are men and buildings are done to order without any thought given to something as boring as a toilet. Also, worktops in kitchen are the optimum height for women yet driving seats in cars and seatbelts are designed for men as standard; there are so few women bricklayers because house bricks are made to fit in male hands comfortably – the standard measurements for so many common or garden items are for male use. What we take for granted is just another form of careless isolation to exclude women from the workplace and to curb our freedoms and bids for equality. Anyway at least we don't have to share our public toilets with men, I guess. I was telling this to Beetroot and Gene at work, and they said I was a moron; Beetroot asked me who on earth gave a zookeeper's fuzzy bum crack about toilets? Then they went on to ask me what 'us birds' wrote on cubicle walls, hazarding idiotic guesses that we most probably swapped recipes for cupcakes and flapjacks, and that there was even a rack in every cubicle where we could all borrow knitting patterns and find handy tips on vaginal hygiene and tampon application. They're a pair of knobs. All they do is fart about and set dumb booby traps for us in the stockroom. Once they put Sellotape across an open doorway just above eye level and we'd accidentally walk into it and get it stuck in our hair, or the other day one of them loosened the cap on my orange juice when I wasn't looking and then I shook it, and it went everywhere. Bell end city or what? I went in the men's loos and wrote, Gene bummed Beetroot – IDT, in one of the stalls.

It's not as much fun here now Rowan has left. The boys just lunch together and wind us girls up. I'm dreading when Astrid goes. She might be going on holiday with her sister to Sicily for a week soon, so she's not got very long left, then she's off to uni to do her Creative Writing BA. I hope Ash invites her to come back in the holidays, but she probably won't want to. Ugh, anyway, I've got to do a few more sketches in preparation for beginning my foundation course still and then I'll submit my final piece and then I'll be also say goodbye to all these slow boats too; goodbye college, goodbye Eton Wick Services.

Gene | That's the way love is…

When I got in from work the other day, my dad was sitting on the driveway in a garden chair. He looked like a faded Polaroid in his cut-off Lees and flip flops; his hairy chest and belly hanging out of his open denim shirt, he was sporting his favourite Aviator sunnies too. I laughed and asked him if he thought he was Greg Allman or someone – he always dresses like a seventies movie private eye when it gets hot outside. He'd been washing the car, and as an afterthought he'd put out bowls of salad, crisps, peanuts, dips, and a few cans of lager cooling in a refreshing looking ice bucket. They were all set out on my old snooker table he'd dragged out of the garage. Dad said he'd been waiting for me to come home and thought it would be a nice surprise. It was, as we don't really cross paths all that often. I sat down and let him tell me about his week, his job, his speculations about QPR's prospects for the next go around, what car he was going to be getting after he'd sold our newly washed Audi. He talked about people falling asleep around the world and what it might mean for everybody. He compared the economic impact to the sanctions the world was imposing on

South Africa, but he lost me quickly. I just replied fuck Botha, and he informed me lightly that someone called FW De Klerk was now the Prime Minister and that he might be one of the good guys as he was talking about dismantling Apartheid. I'm not worried though, he said, there's no sleep to be had, except for when you're in love, and I'm not in love. Dad then got me to have a cold beer with him, he said he couldn't remember ever sitting down and sharing a proper drink with me; I don't drink lager, I like bitter, but I made an exception just to be sociable seeing as he'd obviously put in some effort. He eventually got around to asking me about Rowan, I was impressed he remembered her name as he's only met her once and that was only briefly, coming in together after work one day. I told him quite plainly I'd lost her and I was still quite upset about it – the feeling kept on swimming back unchecked. Dad took a long drink of his beer and crushed the empty can in his hand, burped and shook his head slowly. I don't know what to say, he said. Sometimes it's this simple. She just doesn't want you. She's decided she's not in love with you anymore, and that's if she ever was in the first place. I know it won't make you feel any better but there'll be other girls and you'll lose them too - that's the way love is. I told him thanks and that there was a song we played on the radio show called That's the Way Love Is by Ten City. He asked me if I had a copy, and I didn't. Tonight, when I got in from pissing about with Bob, I found a copy of the import 12" on my bed in a Slough Record Centre bag that he'd gone out and bought for me.

The Chorus | The animal was a fool...

About one year or so before all of the dogs died, my saluki Lulu ran away. This dog gave me trouble from day one, but we still kind of loved her, the boys, my husband Paolo, we all did. But she was insane and so badly behaved; I laughed when she barked and went crazy at a lettuce thinking it was a cat hiding under a car once, she even ate a cheque book.

When Andrea, Luca, and Roberto were children and we still lived in Rimini, they begged me to buy them a puppy. Throughout the entire summer, the autumn, and by Christmas they had worn down my defences – they had me convinced that if I bought them a dog, they would do everything for it. Anyway, in my wisdom, I decided that if my children were obsessed with having a dog, then they'd take good care of it, right? No, I don't think so, I told them. You may think me unkind, but children are not reasonable people. Within a month of the dog's arrival, they'd forgotten it existed; they did not walk her, did not even play with her, I was even the one to name the stupid dog, then they all complained I hadn't chosen the right name for her – why not Killer or Fang they

69 | Cerberus

implored? All they did was kick their football at the dog, push it out of their way, blame their disgusting smells on her, and overfeed her the wrong types of food. No prizes for guessing who became the dog's mamma? In the end, I wound up with four children not three.

Lulu was stupid, very stupid, more stupid than my three little sons as if that was possible; she was a lovable dog, yet the animal was a fool, and more than a bit sly when it came to a food heist. She just used to sit on the couch all day, or bark at noises near the front door. I took her for her walkies twice a day, but sometimes after work, all I could manage was a short trot around the neighbourhood. Anyway, this one particular day, when she was two years old, I had roasted a chicken and I had taken it out of the oven to cool on the side. Lulu at her most daring made a grab for it when she thought the coast was clear. The temptation was too much for her and she had leapt up onto the counter and dragged the chicken to the floor and began to paw at it, yet it was just too hot for her to get her face into. I tried to get a grip of her, but she wriggled out of her collar, and then stood in front of the hot chicken baring her teeth at me, snarling. The children screamed. Luca was clinging to my legs. But Roberto made a dash towards the dog to protect his brothers; this made her dart out through the back door and then we saw her charge down the side of the house through my father's lean-to. This was just as Paolo was coming through the gate in his car and the dog ran into the street, and off into a sprint. I shouted, calling him an idiot before I gave chase like some mad lady, shouting to passers-by to stop her, but the dog just ran and ran. I could see her in the distance, on and on she went, past the city trainyards. I thought she was going to run onto the tracks, but luckily, she didn't see the cut-through hole in the fence where stupid people risked their lives to take a short cut to the city. Paolo was also searching in his car, but he drove the wrong way. After a while I gave up, but we received phone calls and visits from neighbours who told us Lulu had been seen tearing down the middle of some busy street, or by the Marecchia, however nobody could catch her, they said it was like she was running scared. I was very stressed, but the children were in a dreadful state, poor Lulu, they cried. If the dogcatcher caught her, she had no ID on her – I sat on the couch toying with her collar in my hands all night. I woke up in my bed in the early hours with a horrible thought that she had run up a gangplank onto one of the container ships, then I fell asleep dreaming about her being cared for by a young sea hand in his tiny cabin and they lived happily ever after in some far-away place like Buenos Aires. But I saw then that anything could have happened to her. Our hearts began to hurt from what we knew, but they hurt even worse for what they didn't. Her bearings had been completely erased – it was all so stupid.

For days we looked for Lulu but, in the end, I had to accept she wasn't coming home. We thought the dogcatcher had to have caught her, but when we went to the pound, they said no, and when we were shown the dogs that had been rounded up in recent days, Lulu wasn't amongst them; they were some of the saddest specimens I'd ever seen. We had the same result at the vets. The receptionist called me a careless woman and said I should think of the situation from my poor dog's point of view. She inferred the dog had probably been run over by a car or drowned in the Marecchia, but dogs are survivors – what did she know? I told her to go fuck her mother; she seemed to castigate me just because she could but what about my chicken? When, in the end, it dawned on the children that the dog was never going to come back, they became extra sad, but I told them to forget about Lulu and reminded them how they'd neglected their so-called 'sister' and they should learn a lesson from the whole sorry situation. They just blew raspberries at me then went out to play football with their friends.

In the main, I think children have very short memories which doesn't make any sense to me because they haven't been around all that long; they have far less to remember so this should make them much less forgetful right? But as Lulu stayed lost, the weeks went past, and her name became forgotten, her old basket and toys were left out for the rubbish man, her food tipped in the bin – the boy's tears got shed for other reasons – then after a few months Andrea's best friend was given a dog for his birthday and the pestering began all over again. All three boys asked me for a new dog as if Lulu had never existed and this made me feel very sad for the poor and forgotten wretch. So, that time I stood firm and told them no, when they were grownups, they could buy their own dogs. But now there are no dogs, and they hate me because it's too late. They can't have a dog of their own, nobody can, but that's not my fault. The dogs are dead.

Rowan | I didn't make him disappear...

I haven't seen Gene for over a week ever since I saw him off down the road that evening. Ash said he would put us on different shifts which was alright of him. He said it was for his own benefit because he had seen it happen a dozen times - couples who work together breaking up and disrupting everything around them at work. He said dating people you work with never ends well. He loves the sound of his own voice so much. I was eating a cake at the time he was going on about it all and I just wanted to mush it into his idiotic face.

Ash didn't care or react when I told him I'd got a new job at Daniels, he didn't try to change my mind or say I was a hard worker or anything. He did ask me if I knew anyone who could take over my shifts though. I told him to give them to Casey as she was saving up to go to Australia, and he said that was the first he'd heard about it, then he marched off into the back somewhere like I'd said something wrong.

All this makes me wonder how Gene is, I thought he looked shaken when I told him I didn't want to go out with him anymore.

His voice went all tremulous, high and cracked, and I thought he was going to cry, then he went and called me a bitch and threw a rock at me.

I think it's for the best we've split up, but not seeing him at all though, anywhere, afterwards, that's been a surprise – I haven't even seen him in the street. I did see Bob Funkhouse, who crossed the road to avoid me which upset me quite a bit because we'd always had a laugh together. Next Thursday, I'm going to The Trout so I might see Gene there. I don't want to get back together with him, but I want to make sure he's OK. I suspect he'll black me out, but I don't care. I just want to see him, just to make sure I didn't make him disappear – I know that makes me sound like a lunatic, but I can't stop thinking about him now. I shouldn't miss him, as he was a terrible boyfriend, but I do.

Gene | First day of rain...

Bob and I went all the way to Wexham Hospital to see Manjit. We went in Bob's new car, but when we got over to his ward, the nurse told us he'd already been checked out. His mum and dad were looking after him at home, but he still hadn't woken up. He's not on life-support or anything, Mukthar told me, when we were last at Red Shoes FM, he's simply sleeping, it's all as if he'll wake up at any minute. His brain scans match that of somebody who is having a kip, and he's supposedly choosing to be that way which doesn't make all that much sense to me. Their dad was told by the doctors that Manjit's condition was idiopathic, whatever that means; that it is becoming an increasingly and worryingly common problem. Bob pointed to one of the newspapers in the shop at the hospital; the headline said Maggie Philbin from Tomorrow's World has fallen into an unexplained coma just like Manjit had.

The next day, my dad gave me lift to Langley to see Manjit at home. He played this old song by Dexys Midnight Runners called Knowledge of Beauty on the way. I've grown up with that tune; I think it reminds Dad of Mum, but he doesn't say as much - he just hums along to it or stays quiet.

Manjit's mum answered the door and she said he was upstairs sleeping. I asked if I could see him, she paused before letting me inside – I could smell burnt spices. All the rooms were shrouded in gloom because the curtains everywhere were closed. She touched a finger to her lips, led me upstairs and then opened his bedroom door. Manjit was fast asleep like I knew he would be. Seeing him like this made me think back to when we were in primary school together and the teacher would make us play sleeping lions before home time. Dim light from a small lamp on his bedside table was casting a Ready Brek glow around the walls and I could see the rise and fall of his chest. The doctors were right, it looked like he would open his eyes any minute. I felt like a weirdo standing there just looking at him so I set about scanning the room to see if I could see any of the stuff he'd had off me over the years. Up on the shelves near the ceiling, I could see the edges of paint-chipped toy cars, his treasured Martha Cooper and Henry Chalfant graffiti books, old Buntlack spray cans and paint nozzles, a tennis racket, a small guitar amp, and the plush soft toy Pac-Man we used to extinguish lit matches on. Sat on a chest of drawers next to his bed was his brother Mukhtar's prized ghetto blaster that, as kids, we rocked our Whodini, Trouble Funk, and Street Sounds Electro tapes on. We'd lazing in this blanket tent he'd erected in the garden during those bloody long hot summers of '85 and '86. Back when all we did was try to do the human beat box like Buffy out the Fat Boys or rap the words to Hard Times by Run DMC. What a fucking hoot, we'd drink Rola Cola, eat KP Skydivers, make up stories about the girls we fancied, make up lies about the famous people we'd met like Lenny Henry or Knight Rider; sometimes we'd even try to set light to our own farts. Mukhtar once set his jeans aflame because a dangling thread in one of the seams burned up into his crotch – you could see this tiny flame zigzagging through the stitch work; it was hilarious watching him whack himself in the balls to put the fire out – the sheer panic. It still had comedy value up until recently… Whenever he went out for a fag, one of us would say, don't set your pubes on fire, Mukhtar! If he wasn't such a grump, the nickname of Hot Balls might have stuck to him, but he used to punch us or put us in some form of headlock or hold until we went blue or shouted for mercy – it was worse for Manjit as there was no escape – ha ha. You try calling Mukhtar Hot Balls and see what he does.

After a few minutes, his mum made a gesture as if to close the door indicating it was time for me to go. Her English wasn't very good, so I didn't really know what to say to her. I said goodbye, then went back home. Dad hadn't waited, so I ended up walking to the nearby bus stop through the rain. First day of rain in weeks.

Astrid | The thing that you are...

During my breaks at work, I've been reading this book called Beginnings by Ed Datta. One chapter talks about establishing the thing that you/we are, recognising it, and then acting upon it. Although I'm not actually sure I got the full gist of it, it made me wonder whether or not I am already the person or thing I was always going to be? I felt an urgent need to know that my life was exactly what it seemed to be.

Synnøve says there's more than one way of looking at somebody, she told me her lecturer was discussing this as part of an acting module at the dance academy. She said there is the image we portray of ourselves by what we say, how we dress, our perfume, our hair, our attitude, but then there is all the other stuff we try to hide or are simply unaware of that we can't help giving away about ourselves. Synnøve went on a bit about the impassé between how we want to be seen and how we are seen. Makes me think about what people think of me when they see me or talk to me, and whether or not it matches what I'm hoping for in my head. Synnøve's friend Enos said that what other people think of you isn't any of your business. That if you think about that kind of silly shit too much, you'll hold yourself back from doing whatever it is you want to do. But isn't everybody obsessed about what other people think of them? It's all my mates at college and at Eton Wick Services talk about. I always thought, the things we don't know about one another we imagine and make up anyway; we don't like gaps in our pictures of each other.

Synnøve has finally persuaded Mum to allow her to take me on holiday to Sicily with her and some friends. I also asked Lance if he was cool with it too, and he said it was fine by him as long as he could go on his ten-day-long 'weekender' in Ibiza with the Car Freaks. I know what event he's talking about and some of the other lads are going with their girlfriends, so I don't know why Lance won't let me go with him, but I've already said it was OK, because I really want to go to Sicily. Mum went to Sicily a few years ago with her old boyfriend, Ricky, so she knows what it's like out there. She took me out for a Ploughman's Lunch at Parslows in Windsor so she could give me a pep talk; it was like she had a checklist to get through. She more or less told me most men were charming and that although there were nice ones, most of them didn't have our/my best interests at heart at all, they'd use strawberry-flavoured words to get me into bed, and that they may even resort to spiking my drinks or using brute force to get me there; in short, she asked me to stay with Synnøve pretty much the whole time. Then after she'd assured herself I'd got the message, she told me a story about an older guy she met in her twenties called Anders who I'd never heard of before. She ended her tale by telling me there was a difference between a man 'wanting you' and a man 'needing you.' A big fucking difference, she said, and Mum never, ever swears.

Another thing I had to promise to do was to buy and show Mum every book on my first term reading list for university. But that's OK because I own two of them so far, I just need to buy Aristotle's Nicomachean and Eudemian Ethics, John Steinbeck's Tortilla Flat, William Shakespeare's A Midsummer Night's Dream, Edward Abbey's Desert Solitaire, Emma by Jane Austen, The Bell Jar by Sylvia Plath, William S Burroughs' Naked Lunch, Wilfred Owen's Selected Poems, JL Carr's A Month in the Country, Berg by Ann Quin, Montage of a Dream Deferred by Langston Hughes, The Conscience of Words by Elias Canetti, The Sea, The Sea by Iris Murdoch, A Doll's House by Henrik Ibsen, errr I think that's it, oh yeah, and Bent by Martin Sherman. I need to get into a ton of imagist poetry, whatever that is, too. The supplementary reading list contains titles by hundreds of authors, poets and playwrights who I've only heard of in passing like Thomas Bernhard, Clarice Lispector, Lynne Tillman, Andrew Marvell, Mary Wollstonecraft, Madeleine Bourdouxhe, Annie Ernaux, Fernando Pessoa, Natalia Ginzburg, Simone de Beauvoir, Edmund Burke, Joan Didion, Yukio Mishima, Robert Walser, Natéria Friere, David Hare, Janet Malcolm, Chinua Achebe, James Baldwin and Max Frisch. It will cost me over a month's wages to buy the core texts, but I can get some out of the library, but it will save me from going into my student grant for now. I'm to take at least one of them with me to Sicily, Mum said. I've picked the slimmest one, Bent, just so I can take more clothes. We're going next week as soon as Synnøve's term finishes.

When I arrived at the shop yesterday morning for my shift, I had to wait outside for ages because Ash was late with the keys. He said he'd overslept for the first time in his life by an hour. Gene phoned his house and he said it rang about twenty times before anybody picked it up – luckily Parminder had spare keys and she let us inside. Ash has begun to put Gene and Beetroot on at different times because nothing gets done when the two of them are on together. Beetroot isn't even out of his probation period yet, but Ash is desperate for staff, nobody in their right mind would stick around that place for very long. It's majorly boring and Ash, Gene and stupid Beetroot are lemons.

The Chorus | Contained within it all...

The dogs contained within them all the dogs that went before them and all that would come afterwards until the last generation of their kind. Each dog an individual, but unknowably similar like the fractals in snowflakes, ferns, trees, intestines and brains. It's lazy to suspect that they are of the same mind but it's not for me to say or to even toil over. We assume they are the same because they all behave so similarly to one another, yet they do not communicate with words, and we think this makes them a lesser being because they are, perhaps, less keen to express their individuality. All this... Yet the dogs were nothing like us, but we were them, and they were us.

Rowan | Thousands and thousands of crosses...

Mum is the only person I know who ever really talks about the dogs' extinction but it's not as if we don't all know what became of them. Like Gene and the dogs, she's also disappeared, yet I can see her still. She asked me if I thought there was more to her than her mistakes at the breakfast table this morning. I didn't know if she was talking to me or her cereal, so I didn't answer, and I still don't know how to respond now. Perhaps she thinks I'm one of her mistakes.

Mum is the custodian of the Dog Necropolis in Slough. It's situated on the side of the big hillside close to Upton Park; at a crest in the cemetery's high ridge there's a massive statue of a three-headed dog with the words 'breathe another air' carved into its base. There's a console with a big button you can press on its side, and it emits a loud howl which can be heard for miles lasting for thirty seconds. Hope told me the sculpture is of Cerberus, this strange character of ancient myth that guards the gates of Hell. She said she was drawing a tattoo inspired by the monolith. I think a hell dog is a very odd choice for a graveyard anyway, its mixed messages unnerve me – it's full of portent. Maybe the three heads are a twisted representation of the holy trinity. I asked Mum why Cerberus?, and she said the design was selected from an open tender to artists all over the world. She then trailed off, without having answered me, even in part.

Mum does jobs like throwing away dried-out bouquets of flowers or picking up people's rubbish; she mows the grass and strims the path edges and rakes the gravel back onto the walkways from the lawn areas; she undertakes tree and wildflower surveys as well. Being there helps her feel closer to her dogs; on each of their headstones is a photograph of them encased in a glass ball. I think it makes them look like cartoon astronauts, but I don't say this to Mum. She's up there most days keeping it immaculate, I wish she would spend as much time keeping our house tidy.

People say cemeteries are lifeless places but it's the living who make them that way, not those who are buried there. All around you can see life, flowers, summer orchids, visiting birds, tons of insects like ants and spiders, woodlice, foxes.

You can see literally thousands and thousands of crosses in rows across the cemetery's wooded hillside. Mum's Trudy and her other dogs are buried there near to the cemetery's highest point. During the winter you can see the Round Tower of Windsor Castle through the bare branches of the treetops. In the spring, the trees are gorgeous with pink blossom, then they all seem to shed on the same day as if waiting in line for the same gust of wind to undress them.

The Chorus | Loved like no other...

Whenever I got angry and thumped the wall, or stamped my foot out of frustration, Rikki would run under the table and hide out, smiling but panting hard. Did all dogs look like they were smiling when they were frightened and stressed? Her ears pinned back, her mouth would hang open, she looked delirious. I wasn't angry at her, it was just everyday frustration – I'd dropped an egg, made a cup of tea without realising there was no milk in the fridge, lost keys, things like that. Like a child, I'd comfort her, I'd take her in my arms to calm her and to let her know she was loved like no other.

I've only ever had her though, one dog, one life. She was the one for me. I've never understood people who just swap things out. Their dog died, they'd just buy a new one - their husband died, their wife, bam, go out, get a new one. Where is the sense in this? It's callous, just callous. When you're dead you're dead, and there's no coming back – but you can't just pave over a loved one's existence with somebody else. Think about how they'd feel if they miraculously walked in through the front door one day to see another dog in their basket, or another man in your bed, another woman occupying your space like you were never there. Thin vanity – flaccid self-reflection – nothing has a permanence anymore. We're simply addicted to feeling loved, and loving.

Gene | Places to hide...

Bob and I took out some spray cans to The Pit the other night. We ended up staying until sun-up to do this piece dedicated to Manjit. We'd had the idea to go out after watching Black Rain on video for about the nineteenth time, I'm dreading the late-charge fees; it's so good though. We've all been quoting lines from it for the last month and trying yet failing to pause the tape at the exact moment when Andy Garcia gets his head sliced off by the Yakuza bikers. I think the soundtrack is amazing; I usually hate those '80s rock vibes in movies but that opening song, Holding On by Greg Allman, is so good. It's like Rocky or something. Anyway, I can't stop thinking about how deep Black Rain is. Maybe me and Bob will hit Tokyo on a holiday one day. Watch your tail cowboy!

You can find The Pit beneath the old council lorry and bus scrapyard in Chalvey at the end of White Hart Road (near the railway tracks and the M4). Someone has cut a doorway into the chain link fence; you can peel a section back and climb through it with ease. There are loads of places to hide in amongst the rusty buses, vans, and old refuse trucks, most of which have been decorated with small throw ups and tags. Anybody who went looking around in there would have trouble finding you – there's literally acres of trucks parked in a herring bone zig-zag pattern. There are no cocky watchmen there, at least we've never seen one, and there's no such thing as a guard dog anymore. There are these old video cameras up on posts around the edge of the plot but I'm pretty sure they're dead. Who wants to guard this horrible pile of old buses anyway? There are literally dozens of them falling apart all over the site – some are inside a semi-circle of four hoop barns and random sheds – others have been left to the elements under the boughs of sickly looking trees and bushes. In some cases, the foliage is growing up from out of a vehicle – saplings growing up out of the soil left behind from nests or bird shit and fly-tipped garden waste.

At the far end of the main depot there is a wide staircase down to The Pit itself – its doors hanging off their hinges. They are beyond lines of smashed up portacabins that had once been wheeled inside to stand as offices for the site boss and his admin staff most probably. In the gloom, there are unseen perils like mechanics' pits to fall down and discarded ramps, jacks, tyre irons to trip over – it's some seriously scary shit if you go down there half-drunk. You can almost always hear pigeons cooing as you walk around and the sounds of running water like an underground stream or drain. We have an established 'safe route' to The Pit now – someone from somewhere has spray painted big yellow arrows on to a few of the trucks, so you don't die by misadventure or get lost forever in there – you skulk around in the maze half-expecting the Minotaur to pop out!

I always think the doorway down to The Pit looks like a fucked-up face especially since a random graff artist, maybe Slave, has painted two giant yellow eyes across the space between the top of the doors and the ceiling making the doorway look like a weird mouth. Whoever did it has daubed the words, As Above So It Is Below, in something that looks like tar on the royal blue doors. There's no sign anymore of the chains and padlocks that should've been on the double doors to keep us out.

Down beneath the depot, The Pit itself is this huge high-ceilinged, concrete cavern about the size of the school hall at Windsor Boys. At its centre, the expansive floor slopes upwards to the rim of a huge bowl. From the lip of the bowl, you can see flood tunnels fanning out from its base below. The bottom of the pit is almost always ankle-deep in drifts of dead leaves, fizzy drink cans and crisp packets. If you run down the edge of the bowl to the bottom, you can follow the tunnels away into the blackness for a few metres before your way is blocked by gratings; you have to crouch down or go on all fours to move through them, they're kind of like funnels; you wouldn't want to go down there though – there's all kinds of things caught in the gratings - mud, dead animals, bog roll, soaked car magazines, pornos, people piss in there and worse, so it stinks. If you were to shout down them, you'd get funny echoes and sound distortions but it gives me a chill so I don't like to do it. There is a gallery with railings running around the lip of the bowl which makes it easy to climb in and out of simply by grabbing hold of them. There's also some kind of radial gantry going out to the centre of the circle; at the end of the catwalk is a wrecked console with its wiring pulled out and its screen smashed - me and Bob don't have a clue what the bowl's purpose was or is. Most of the time, the only sound down there is the distant dripping of water that increases after a rainy spell, then you'll hear a rush, like a small waterfall. The only living things down below are rats, trapped birds, and the odd detouring rabbit – you hear them scratching their claws or flapping their wings, you don't ever really see them unless they've died.

We always take our torches with us or there is no point in going. There's no light down there except whatever gets in through the smashed occulus windows high up in the walls; most of them were boarded up but in places the planks have fallen away. The windows are really slats and when you are outside, they are at shin height. You can't get out through any of the windows as they're too high and several trucks are parked snug up to the wall leaving no room to slip your way under and out. If we're planning a night of it, Bob will bring this industrial work light his dad owns which works as a pretty powerful floodlight, but most of the time, we're on the fly and only visit on a spur of the moment; that's when we have to rely on the smaller but still half-decent torches we keep in our backpacks. A while back, probably two or three years ago, some older kids burnt a load of wooden pallets and tyres in the centre of the bowl, and you can still see the charred black shapes left by the fire and smoke on the concrete ceiling and walls. There was hardly anywhere for the smoke to get out, so whoever did it must have just run off and watched from outside, I don't know. This might have been back before the dog murals started to appear though, back when graff round here was exclusively made up of crap like football team names, NF, Combat 18, ALF, swastikas, other racist bollocks, gay slurs, crap bubble writing, the word 'break!' as well as lots of cartoon dicks and boobies.

Everywhere you go in The Pit, you can see the vast dog murals looming out of the darkness at you. There must be about two dozen at least – there's dogs ten-foot-tall, lofty and wide, running, galloping, eating, winking, dressed like rappers with giant clock faces dangling from fat gold chains around their necks, buoyant basketball kicks on their paws. Others are really artistic portraits; these are the ones we like the best, the ones by Slave – they are usually accompanied with some poetry or a short quote – then there'll be the eulogies. The messages are like howls with no voice.

Mongo, RIP

Lady, rest in Paws

Bonnie, we miss you

Dumbo, we love you

Cheesy, come back

Bonnie, RIP

You aren't dead, just having a long kip, Bonny

God bless and cherish Nigel

Missy, rest in peace

Mirabelle, where did you go?

Duke, I will never stop loving you

Tonga, u were my world

Aubrey, what will I do without you?

Deke - You are missed

Caleb, never forgotten

Kipper FETCH!

Sherbet, come home

Alice, sleep princess
Beau, my mate
Nothing without you, Froofer
In the arms of God, Spike
Goodbye Tommy
Milko - you were my medic
For Mum - Trudy, Meg, and Griff. We miss you, every day.

At the beginning of the summer, I took Astrid, Casey and Nutty Snacks to The Pit. We were all having a good day at work, having a laugh and just arsing about – there was none of the sass and attitude they give me most days. It actually felt like we were all a bunch of mates and it was us against Ash and the customers – it didn't last – they were crabby and moody as ever the next day. Anyway, that was when I suggested to them to come with me down The Pit after work. Rowan ducked out at the last minute but the other three followed along. Astrid pulled out this old Polaroid camera out of her bag. I didn't think the pictures would come out very well, but I was wrong because the camera flash was really strong and worked wonders. She said she'd found herself bewitched by the dogs down there, said it all reminded her of the wallpaper at Rowan's house, and she was right. Nutty Snacks and Astrid said they wanted to come back and take reels of photos of the lorries and buses, I don't know if they ever did. They never said anything to me about it.

Bob spends a lot of his time down in The Pit looking for discarded spray cans, hoping they've been abandoned rather than depleted so he can add pieces of his own to the gallery. Bob was three years old when all the dogs dropped dead, but he claims to remember his pet corgi, Vivah, clearly. The first spray can portrait he completed down in The Pit was copied from a picture of her that he borrowed from the altar his mother and father had assembled at their home to their pet's memory. It's not very good, he's way better at letter shapes and drawing ghetto blasters.

About eight of the murals are by the mysterious Slave. I know some painters that travel miles to bomb a decent site, yet Bob and I have never encountered a single other soul down in The Pit apart from those we went in with. There's never anybody. I wonder about the people who have been down there to draw, who they are or were. Why dogs? I guess I'll never find out.

The other night, we set up stall at the entrance to Tunnel 302; the five storm drains running out of the pit are numbered 301 to 306 (there is no 304). Bob got out his letter templates and we worked on an outline of the words, Wake Up Manjit! It was teal and electric mauve with lightning bolts coming out of it. We also put Red Shoes Radio - 90.7 FM and the name of The M Brothers House Party radio show and the time it went out followed by our tags, 3rd Rail (me) and Predator. By the time we'd wrapped it all up, we could see daylight coming in through the gaps around the big doors leading back to the dead lorries.

The Chorus | It's Like That Y'all…

(The M Brothers Militant Mixdown© featuring DJ Bob Funkhouse - Red Shoes FM – 90.7 FM - 08/08/1990)

Get, get, get busy y'all. This is the M Brothers Militant Mixdown giving you something funky dope for the nine-oh with a show full of hype jams to keep you on the floor. Don't forget to come to The Slammer on the 13th of August - ring the number you already have and if you don't have it ask a friend, ask that bad ragamuffin at the bus stop, ask your sister, ask your woman, ask that dirty old ho in the alley, ask your girlfriend, ask your imam, everybody is going to be in the place. Even your mum is going to be there, it's that large. You best believe. Rudeboys, B-Belles, big, tall, skinny, fat, black, white, brown, yellow, red, green, purple, Punjabi, Bengali, Maori, Jamaican, Nigerian, Swedish, Israelian, Persian, posho, Kev, Sharon - let's all give peace a dance. We got the M Brothers on deck supported by the man like Bob Funkhouse, Boodlal the Beast, Ashton the Ragamuffin Don Dadda Dragon, Amina Allure, Special Brew dancer Johnny Double Glazing and the Bad Sex Twins – Nita and Thomasina. This one is going out to

Manjit who is working his way past a long lie down… We miss you bruv and we will be spinning your favourite tunes at the event and on this show each and every Saturday night – play it loud and proud earwigging posse. Send us your requests – we have the man like Jazzy Gene and the one, Beetroot Brian, on the phones, so respect is due, overdue and crucial. On the show, we have an essential Bob Funkhouse mix – tonight it's a hip hop showdown featuring a load of 12"s we picked up at Mega Mega, Slough Record Centre, and the cosmic Revolution Records in Windsor. Give them shops your support – they love you, we love them. There's so much L.O.V.E. in Berkshire right now. We want all those with sleepers in the house to turn the radio up… We want your brothers, sisters, mums, dads, girlfriends, boyfriends, sons, daughters, hoes, bitches, gangsters, pimps, pushers, gamblers, prozzies, plonkers, everybody, all alive and hopping. No more sleeping, get your dirty butts out of those beds for real. Reeeeeeeewind.

First on deck, we got a Hacienda classic, Carino by T-Coy. Like we even need to introduce a track like that… Stop the nonsense. And, oh yeah, Whitney Houston, if you're listening, I'm still saving ALL my love for you, just don't tell Linda Lusardi. Peace.

T Coy - Carino | **Mike Dunn** - Life Goes On | **The KLF presents The JAMS** - Whitney Houston Joins the JAMs | **Fast Eddie** - Acid Thunder | **Bou Khan** - It's Magic | **Tony G** - Tony's Song | **Electra** - Jibaro | **Joe Cuba** - El Pito | **11:59** - T-Minus-60 | **Ice T** - You Played Yourself | **Sweet Tee** - It's Like That Y'all | **Dynamix II (feat. Too Tough Tee)** - Give The DJ a Break | **Shut Up and Dance** - Lamborghini (remix) | **Above The Law** - Untouchable |

LL Cool J - Jinglin' Baby (remix) | **Heavy D & The Boyz** - We Got Our Own Thang | **Hijack** - The Badman is Robbin' | **Think Tank** - A Knife and a Fork | **Big Daddy Kane** - Young Gifted and Black | **Lord Alibaski** - Top Gun | **Demon Boyz** - International Karate | **Caron Wheeler** - Livin' In The Light | **Massive Attack** - Daydreaming | **Grandmaster Flash** - Girls Love The Way He Spins | **Cutmaster DC** - Brooklyn Rocks The Best | **Boys Next Door** - Imperial Scratch | **David Bowie** - Let's Dance (Put On Your Red Shoes) | **Johnny Nash** - There Are More Questions Than Answers | **En Vogue** - My Lovin' | **Curtis Mayfield** - We Are The People Darker Than Blue | **Audio Two** - On the Road Again | **Stezo** - To The Max | **Three Times Dope** - Mr Sandman | **Young MC** - Bust a Move | **James Brown** - My Thing | **Maceo & The Macks** - Across The Tracks | **JVC FORCE** - Smooth and Mellow | **Melba Moore** - Make Me Believe In You | **Joyce Sims** - All and All (UK remix) | **The Knights of The Turntables** - Techno Scratch | **Today** - I Got Da Feelin' | **Teddy Riley (feat. Guy)** - My Fantasy | **MC Shan** - Juice Crew Law | **Aleem (feat. Leroy Burgess)** - Release Yourself (dub) | **Sir Ibu of Divine Force** - The Peacemaker | **The DOC and Dr Dre** - The DOC & The Doctor | **Def Jef** - Droppin' Rhymes on Drums | **Just Ice** - Back to The Old School | **Deee-lite** - Groove is in the Heart | **New Order** - Shellshock | **Biz Markie** - Spring Again | **Master Ace & Action[3]** - I Got Ta | **Tyree** - Acid Over | **2 Puerto Ricans, A Black Man & A Dominican** - Do It Properly | **Chad Jackson** - Hear the Drummer Get Wicked | **Pet Shop Boys** - I Want a Dog | **Isaac Hayes** - Joy | **Idris Muhammad** - Loran's Dance | **Doug Carn** - Suratal Ihklas | **James Brown** - The Big Payback | **King Tee & Mixmaster Spade**

- Ya Better Bring a Gun | **DJ Jazzy Jeff & The Fresh Prince** - Brand New Funk | **Lakim Shabazz** - All True and Living | **Curtis Mayfield and Ice T** - The Return of Superfly | **Mellow Man Ace** - Hip Hop Creature | **Ultimate Force** - I'm Not Playing | **Levi 167** - Something Fresh To Swing To | **Boogie Down Productions** - Why Is That? | **Trouble Funk** - Drop the Bomb | **Chubb Rock & Howie Tee** - Caught Up (remix) | **The 45 King (feat. Lakim Shabazz)** - The Red, The Black, The Green | **Charles B & Adonis** - Lack of Love | **Turntable Orchestra** - You're Gonna Miss Me | **Beloved** - The Sun Rising | **Raze** - Break 4 Love | **808 State** - Cubik | **Frankie Knuckles & Satoshie Tomiie** - Tears | **Vicious Base (feat. DJ Magic Mike)** - Drop The Bass II | **Byron Davis & the Fresh Krew** - My Hands Are Quicker Than The Eye | **Jazzy Jay** - Def Jam | **Unique 3** - Weight of the Bass (3 Ton Mix) | **Newcleus** - Automan | **Man Parrish (feat. The Freeze Force Crew)** - Boogie Down Bronx | **Juggy** - Oily | **Xavier Cugat** - Perfidia | **New Edition** - Pass the Beat | **Zapp** - More Bounce to The Ounce | **George Clinton** - Atomic Dog | **Sterling Void & Paris Brightledge** | It's Alright

Alright tape deck posse, this a rudeboy takeover, repeat, this is a rudeboy takeover. Spread them words, dub them tapes, give them out to your friends, make a list of these tunes, pester the man like Richard at Revolution to get them for you on the wax. There's a dance movement out there, and the stomp of feet is gonna wake the sleeping, it's gonna be so loud the castle walls in Windsor will shake. Even The Queen will be rocking out, man. Make some noise Berkshire, I'm serious, we ain't taking no shorts. Red Shoes

FM in full E F F E C Teee Boyeeeeeeeeeeeeeeeeeeee! M Brothers with Bob Funkhouse in hostage taker mode and don't you forget it. Till next time, stay awake and keep this mutha-bumping frequency clear. Easy… Easy.

Rowan | Confidence of the properly ignorant

Since I've started at Daniels in the bed sales department, I've been talking a lot to my supervisor Warren about different things. He seemed to be easier to talk to than most and I liked him to begin with. Up until the last week or so he'd been giving me a lift back to Eton Wick because he lives over in Taplow or Burnham somewhere, but I did something that made him change overnight; not sure I care all that much about it at the moment but it wasn't all that sensible.

Warren's a fair bit older than me – late twenties, early thirties. I've been telling him about how I'd broken up with Gene and how it feels like he's suddenly stopped existing. Warren told me I was pretty lucky as bust-ups can be a bit hellish and messy. I guess I am kind of grateful Gene isn't hanging around buying me stuff and moping about or worse, turning psycho. But at the same time, it's like a hole in the earth has opened up and swallowed him.

For a short while, a matter of days really, I kept on hoping Warren would make a pass at me, I felt like he'd be about to but then he'd change course. However, he's married, and even though he's gone as far as admitting that he likes me in 'that' way, he also told me that in the eyes of God and the law he's unavailable. That having an extra-marital sexual friendship can only lead to one of two places, nowhere or destruction – is he being fucking dramatic or what? He says he's in love with his wife Gracieuse; she's this Senegalese woman who works mornings on the scarves section. She is very attractive and always wears colourful head scarves and pashminas. She has the smoothest voice with this thick French accent. Warren went on to say he couldn't possibly betray her and that the way he felt was no reflection on me. Also, he knew one relationship was very much like any other, and good people like him and me didn't go around destroying healthy marriages for fun, there were big consequences. I know exactly what he means, but he just wouldn't shut up, on and on he went like I was missing the point; he gave me no credit at all. In the end, I considered myself fortunate I hadn't just got off with this old bore. He really overthinks stuff and states things with the confidence of the properly ignorant, which really puts me off him. Maybe he just likes hearing himself sound off like he's a wise old wizard. I mean, I'm not stupid, I don't want to ruin someone's marriage over a kiss or something; he rounded off one of his sermons by saying things like an indiscretion always have a way of coming out. Resentments, jealousy and hurt, and that there was no such thing as strings-free sex no matter what anybody says (I cringed when he said the word 'sex'). He reckons it's because you can only ever account for yourself and you have no control over the outcome because it involves a second person and at the end of the day, how well do 'we' really know anyone? I think he concluded with a pearl of wisdom that went, if the fear of being found out and losing your partner is the only reason you don't cheat, then that's a good enough reason for you not to cheat. If having a dad is like this then, wow. What a dullard, I thought he might have been fun to begin with but not now.

The last time Warren gave me a lift home, I lifted my skirt and flashed my knickers at him as I was getting out of his car just to put an end to his lectures – I just did it. The next day, he made up an excuse about having to do errands in future on the way back home and I'd have to find another lift from then on. Men are just like boys, falling over their fetid dicks and acting like children. If he'd made a pass at me in some field, like Luca did to that Helen woman, I wouldn't have told anybody, I'd have just chalked it up to experience. I can keep my mouth shut. Who gives a shit, right? But no, now he's giving me vibes and can't look me in the eye when we talk. Maybe it's for the best I didn't try anything on after all.

The Chorus | Listening to this…

I was listening to this new book, All The Pretty Houses by Cormac McCarthy being read on Radio 4 by Mandy Patinkin. It contained a passage where the rancheros were musing on the mysteries of life; they said all horses (perhaps the character in the story was including all animals) are of the same soul, but I don't think they are.

The Chorus | State of disorder...

Dogs weren't here for us; we were here for them – yet people still don't see this. Our dominance as a species has always been the key to our downfall, and the advantage to this kind of delusion means the blame always lies elsewhere.

The world is poorly organised I think, but is it that way by design? I like to see it like this; society is run by a club, only a few people know of its existence. This cabal deliberately mis-manages world affairs into a constant and natural state of disorder. Whether consciously or not, every instinct in our society follows a plan to benefit those at the top but this club works it so the system benefits those at its apex with all the accidents, spontaneity, and coincidences still factored in and intact. If you follow the money, you'd ultimately find out exactly who was behind both the death of the dogs and this new sleeping pandemic. Who is set to gain the most in this set of circumstances? However, the who is not the thing; let us forget about unmasking these shadows for a minute, you know who put us here in the first place, you already know – it's proving their existence and their connection to the mayhem that's harder. If you draw the scenario inside out to fit your answer within a canonical paradigm, it's not so much the 'who' but the 'proof' of the puppet masters' existence that you will need to establish instead – check the patterns and level of repletion. Do you understand? You have to establish their presence – that's the bottom line. And it's all to do with money and know how – they don't want you rich and their ultimate aim is to cut off all the access to information itself.

They wield their power through numbers. It's all numbers and there's a finite number of configurations meaning all the conditions, as chaotic as they are, are exactly right for all members of this clique of criminals to win their game and win it at all costs. All we know, as the days pass, is that the majority of us are losing – and that's even more proof of this cabal's existence. Perhaps that's all the proof any of us need.

Gene | Could she sense something…?

I sat down with Simon P whilst the skateboarders did their thing on the old barn foundations by the Stairway to Heaven. They were playing Megadeth's Holy Wars on the ghetto blaster and doing finger flip tricks off a ramp they'd thrown together. I was pretty impressed by their organisation; one of the really young kids had a broom and had been made to sweep the concrete floor around the half-tube so the skateboarders would get a smooth approach to the jump off. They did stunts like hopping down from the top of the ziggurats onto a pile of mummified mattresses – we watched one guy try to skateboard down a plank somebody had leant off the back of the Stairway to Heaven and they landed on their back but they were OK.

I've got to say, I love the way skateboarders just throw any old shit together onto a cassette tape and just get away with it. I used to loathe the kids at school who weren't aligned to a particular music scene; they never dug any deeper than the commercial Top 40 rundown, but these skater guys, they get a pass from me – it's all deep stuff. They carry it off – I think they are effortlessly eclectic and free of all the bullshit conventions we subject ourselves to just to fit in somewhere, that's kind of the credos or loose dogma of their tribe – they draw vibes from everywhere. I don't usually listen to shit like Slayer or Megadeth but it's pretty persuasive all the same, I'm slowly getting into it, but then again if you weren't into what was playing you knew you didn't have to wait long to find out what was next on their tape and you'd always be surprised. I recognised tracks like Hallelujah by The Happy Mondays, Devotion by Ten City, Eight Legged Groove Machine by The Wonder Stuff, Eat The Menu by The Sugarcubes, This is the One by The Stone Roses, BVSMP's I Need You, Kariya's Let Me Love You For Tonight, The Todd Terry Project's Weekend, Ain't My Type of Hype by Full Force, Mike Dunn's Life Goes On, 20 Seconds to Comply by Silver Bullet, Good Life by Inner City – serious fucking tunes, Anyone by Smith & Mighty, Fishbone's Freddie's Dead, Slayer's South of Heaven tape got played too, and I don't even check for that kind of shit. Sorry, I could reel tunes off for hours and I will. If you don't like my music, then (raspberry).

Most of the skate kids we were sat watching were drinking stolen Lucozade they'd bought from Beetroot. I listened as Simon talked about the news, about people falling asleep all over the place, having accidents, huge motorway pileups, and shoppers found kipping in the aisles at closing time and silly shit like that. Every day, marches were converging on Parliament up in London, and there were student demos up and down the country. He also spoke of rumours that the army were getting primed to crush us. Simon confessed to me he'd always felt tired, all his life as far back as he could remember anyhow, but that he'd fight to stay awake with drugs and his good looks.

Simon smokes a lot, swallows stolen prescription drugs by the ton, and inhales and sniffs toxic shit like nitrous oxide, crap I wouldn't have anything to do with in three lifetimes, but he still says some deep stuff. He's self-appointed himself as The Teacher just like KRS One, as he is always kicking the ballistics and actual-factual-supernaturals to the younger skaters, and because they're all about five years or so younger than him, they kind of look up to him. Some of the pro sponsors used to come and watch him, that's what he told me anyway, but he turned them all down because he became a dad and transferred his love and focus to his son, Roscoe. His girlfriend, Erica, is pretty hot. She was the first person who ever snogged me; we were walking to the shop to buy more beers for a house party we were at, and we were talking about this and that going down along this road in Maidenhead, joking and shit, and out of the blue she dared me to kiss her; this was about, I don't know, two years ago. Anyway, I laughed and said, I'm not kissing you. So, she headbutted this tree trunk really hard, she was embarrassed I'd said no I think, so I asked her why she'd do such a crazy thing, her forehead was bleeding, so I took off my bandana and helped her wipe up the trickle of blood running down her face. When we got to the shop, she stole a packet of plasters and a tube of mints, but we bought the beers. Anyway, Erica ended up kissing me in the 7-Eleven car park out front as if to prove a point, and even now I can still recall the buzz of the neon lights and its green and orange lights reflected in the lenses of her aviator-style glasses. It lasted for days, it was a slow intense kiss. Someone was playing Take My Breath Away from a parked car nearby; I'm not lying to you – the stupid snog song from Top Gun really was pumping out in the distance. That first kiss felt electric, I wish I had the right words to do it justice. I remember my tongue giving the extra strong mint wedged inside her lip, down in front of one of her lower canine teeth a graze and then it was all I could taste, small details bring it back. I never kissed or touched her again after that and we never spoke about it either. I don't know why people kiss you then kill you off. Did she see something in me she didn't like? Could she sense something was off?

Hope | Into his sleeping…

There's a heatwave coming, my dad says. At the factory he runs, he said people have taken to sleeping through their lunchbreaks, sleeping in the bays. He can hear the alarm clocks going off all over the factory. He does empathise though, because he said there have been days this week when he too has needed to draw the blinds in his office and rest his head on the desk. Kath, the CFO, makes him coffee just to keep him going but Dad told me she is drinking just as much caffeine as he is. The heat makes the staff go all slow, he's tried to help but there are massive waiting lists for cooling units to buy or rent. He stocks the fridges and freezers with ice cream, ice packs, and bottles of water but the staff still whinge. I guess that's people though isn't it.

Mum said some of the girls at work are to be seconded to help out at the temporary hospital they've built at Windsor Racecourse to take in all those who can't stay awake.

Carmine's still hasn't reopened but Andrea has returned from Italy to reopen his salon. He's acting the same as he always has – placing bets for customers, drinking wine, watching girls.

I still have a book Luca lent to me; he said it was one of his all-time favourites. It's called My Life With a Star by Jiri Weil, which is about this old Jewish guy in Prague who gets ignored by the Nazis who are putting everybody on the trains to the concentration camps. His name doesn't appear on any of the soldiers' lists, so they keep on sending him away whenever he turns up at the station. It's sad but he doesn't realise he has been spared by a twist of administrative fate. It's very good, I was looking forward to sharing my thoughts with Luca about it, what I'd gleaned from it and to learn from his opinions, but he'd died by then. Now I have nobody to discuss books with, I could talk to Astrid, but she doesn't really know how to talk about the stories – she talks about technique and structure rather than the emotions, the plots and the inner life of the characters. I don't want to know how a tale has been built or about the mechanisms of the story. She's too academic; I just want to talk about the stories as if they were real, discuss the character's feelings and motives.

It was Luca's passing that reminded me I needed to finish it. I will go to Prague someday, but I am worried about flying at the moment, worried about falling asleep in a foreign country. On the news last night, there was a bulletin saying that many airlines are to take on board an extra co-pilot now for safety in case one of the pilots needs to emergency-sleep on the long haul. I think this thing is getting serious.

On Tuesday, I found a black cat in a deep sleep – I couldn't wake it. The sleepy little thing was out on the lane out by the Stairway to Heaven and the half-tube the skaters built. I stroked it for a bit; it had a collar with an address on it that wasn't far away. When I got to the cat owner's house, this old lady answered the front door. She was so happy to see her pet but sad at the same time. The woman was grateful I'd found her Tom Kitten (she called it), but at the same time she was dismayed to see he was fast asleep. The old lady held Tom Kitten up in front of her, his paws dangling, and looked into his sleeping face. She made me wait on the doorstep for a minute or so as she took the animal inside – she came back with a packet of custard creams to say thanks. I took them as I didn't want to be rude, plus I was a little bit hungry, and it was my turn to cook for Mum and Dad that night and I tried unsuccessfully to get away with making them spaghetti hoops on toast.

The Chorus | When the dogs died...

When the dogs died, a large number of their human companions took an oath of silence. They tried as hard as they could to remain muted. Some still haven't uttered a single word since 1975 – they found out there's nothing left to say – it's a deep silence of disgust, of disappointment, of sadness. A pristine quiet like that of a desert.

Rowan | A baby's head…

A guy called Kevin Watmore who worked down in the goods bay at Daniels got fired the other day for loading a brand-new stolen pushchair into a friend's car – straight off the shopfloor and into the dock it went. That was the same day this girl on the home-audio section passed me a note from him saying, I think you're the best-looking girl in Daniels, with love and unity from Fresh Kev, followed by a winking smiley.

Kev is definitely not fresh – he wears this little brown anorak that makes him look like a Coco Pop and he's about four foot tall and these days he has a weasel's moustache, and shoulder-length curly hair like Graeme Souness. He's as thick as pig shit too, he was in all the bottom sets when we were at school. I remember in biology, when we were all having an anatomy lesson with Mrs Cardew – there was this giant diagram of a naked woman Blu-tacked to the blackboard. She pointed to the area between the giant nude's legs with her wand and asked Kev what he thought it was. There was a long pause before he said he thought the woman's bush was a baby's head – just two words were uttered 'baby's head'.

Within seconds the class died in a gale of riotous laughter and even Mrs Cardew had to excuse herself. We could see her doubled over, laughing in the hallway, covering her mouth with her cupped hands. For days afterwards, kids were just saying the words 'baby's head' with Kev's dopey voice to make each other laugh. Kev loved it though – he loved the fame and infamy. He'd even go up to people and say, baby's head, to get a reaction before getting a punch in the arm or being told to drop dead. I remember, all the time, Kev would get bollocked for talking in class, or for his ridiculous answers to questions, or being late for school. The only thing Fresh Kev was good at was football, it was his only talent. Whenever we were in the languages block (which was next to the football pitch) we'd watch him as he wove his way in and out of the other kids on the field with smooth ease; he could outrun and outsmart any opponent when he was on the ball. It's like he had sticky feet, the ball loved him. He stood out because of his lack of stature, his speedy deftness, and his outsized, dirty kit and rotten football boots – I don't think his parents ever had any money. He lived in the high-rise flats over in Dedworth and slept on the balcony in the summer for kicks. His mum was a dinner lady at a primary school (I think), and his dad worked in The Three Elms pub near Trevelyan. He was this big, thick-set Scotsman called Johnny who had swastika tattoos on his forearms and ACAB on his knuckles – bit of a cliche. I still see him out and about now.

I don't know who put 'Fresh Kev' up to writing that note to me, but it made me smile a bit purely because it was typical Kev, it was so out of whack with reality – why on earth would I consider going out with such a birk? I'd sooner take Gene back.

The Chorus | Leaving the body…

Nobody notices pain leaving the body even if its presence has been so bad that it's overruled everything else and become an inanimate object in itself. Its disappearance isn't like when you flick a light off in a room, where you notice it's no longer light; the realisation is more akin to missing how and when the light dimmed without you witnessing it. I think grief works the same way; you don't notice quite how the sensation of loss recedes or the moment your real-life distractions begin to seep back in to replace the feelings of hurt and confusion. I think this is how we all tried to cope with the extinction of our dogs all those years ago. I sense it as something more akin to a haunting. With this sleeping sickness it seems like we're being led back into some pretty surreal pastures once again, and maybe this time there's no way out.

The Chorus | I Want a Dog...

Neil Tennant out of the Pet Shop Boys said that's what led him to write I Want a Dog, his yearning for a loyal four-legged canine companion. It was released during Dog Remembrance Week in 1988 and was number one in the charts for two months, it even came back as a Christmas number one. The pop promo is made up of a montage of old film footage of dogs caught on camera – you must have seen it. I can't stop singing its melody and I do too; I want a dog.

Astrid | If everything goes to plan…

Whilst I was at work today, Synnøve was visiting ours and she said she'd help me pack my suitcase for Sicily. As I suspected, she went and picked out the stuff she's helped me buy in the shops or things she bought me for my birthday or at Christmas. She doesn't really know I've grown a dress size so I can't fit into many of them all that much, although I do really love her taste.

For the second time recently, none of us could get into the shop. It was Casey's day off and Ash was very late. Again, Parminder had to let us all in, and he eventually showed up at nine instead of seven. We had a lot of catching up to do, especially sorting out the newspapers and putting the floats in; usually Ash has done all this for us in advance by the time we turn up. He didn't have a lot to say, he didn't even apologise to us. He looked awful, his hair hadn't been gelled and his breath smelt of old food which is pretty strange for Ash because he really looks after himself and cares about his appearance. He hadn't even shaved. He was very quiet all day, and only smiled once at something he saw in a newspaper. He was even lazier than Gene and Beetroot, who took advantage of the situation by stocking shelves at mega-slow speeds. I said to Lance again about Beetroot's bad attitude and, predictably, he just gave me the brush off.

After work, I went along with the Car Freaks to Winter Hill and we chatted on the radios and then played tunes on our speakers, I chose Knowledge of Beauty by Dexys Midnight Runners, which is mine and Lance's slow song I suppose. I only go out there to watch the sun go down if it's a warm evening – it's the best high view around for miles. Lance enthused about his future life plans - he's hoping to buy a van soon and he wants to go to Newquay to learn how to surf and make cool chains, pendants and necklaces for men and women. He said I could go with him, but I have university – maybe I could join him next summer if everything goes to plan.

That evening, Beetroot brought Hope along. It was nice to see her, but I don't really understand what she sees in him at all. They looked pretty cool together in their long leather coats, even though it's way too hot to be dressed like Batman at the moment. I suppose you don't get to see what attracts a person to someone else because you don't get to see everybody up close. I do tend to wonder if I've missed something in my own assessments; so, when a good friend hooks up with someone I don't like, I'll tend to give their new partner a kind of second chance. Most of the time, I find my first opinion was the one I should have stuck to, but there have been a few notable exceptions over the years. Hope's pretty smart, but I'm sorry, so far Beetroot makes me cringe and recoil whenever I think about him. Perhaps she can persuade him to toss that rotten notebook of his away and give himself a good wash. Why do boys have to be so gungy?

They do look happy together, but he keeps on patting or scratching the top of her head with the tips of his fingers like she's a cat or something. She doesn't seem to mind and responds by putting her arm around him or cuddling into his shoulder. That tickling routine would wear thin with me very quickly. He was doing it every few minutes when they were just standing around with the others; it was as if he had this constant need to remind her he was in attendance – that she belonged to him. I don't know, but it's a bit twee and moronic for my tastes. I can't bear to be touched in public, much as I love Lance.

Synnøve is a bit worried about Sicily because of the increasing numbers of people out there who have fallen asleep. We have been warned to take travel insurance although we can't afford this new 'sleep cover' that is coming into force. We might not even get away now because although the airlines are honouring flights which have been booked in advance, prices are rocketing as there are fewer pilots willing to do more than one flight per day and it'll probably become law soon. Crap Craig was saying aviation fuel prices are likely to come down though so the market may well become less volatile – I don't even know what he's going on about. I'm more worried about the constant demonstrations in London. The government isn't giving anybody answers and a few of the girls are saying they are going to let us all die like the dogs did fifteen years ago. What about all the other animals though? What about the fish? Mum said fishing boats are coming in with empty holds, but I don't know where she got that from, nobody else has said it. But then, I don't even want to turn the TV on anymore, every time I do, I just see the panic, the fights breaking out all around the world. Yet life seems to go on as normal round here, in Eton Wick, Windsor, Slough. You see the occasional people sleeping at their tables in cafés, pubs, others being asked to move on, or being taken away by volunteers to the Windsor racecourse hospital in those green makeshift ambulances – but all this? It's just background.

It's pretty confusing to know the right thing to do, but it will be OK. I've begun to keep a diary, it's one of the things we are required to do in preparation for our degree so we can get used to writing all the time, also we have to jot down new words all the time. It sounds obvious but your average English person has a vocabulary in the region of two hundred and fifty words and the average reading age of a nine-year-old. Compared to all the words in existence, that's a salt cellar's worth compared to a beach's.

Hope | Cheeba cheeba all the time...

Beetroot took me to Winter Hill to meet some of his mates a few days ago. Astrid and Lance were there too but I only really saw them to wave at in the distance. Beetroot was showing off his speakers, he was playing that song by Mantronix called Got to Have Your Love on a loop – I hear that song in my dreams; seriously, it's everywhere at the moment. On the way back home, he gave me half an 'e' and we ran around this field in the dark for ages, it was so warm out, and we fell down and just laughed and talked about the guys we knew and music, places we wanted to go to, and the buzz we felt. He told me certain drugs would keep the whole world awake and amphetamines could have saved the dogs from extinction if the government had considered a dynamic political way of dealing that Beetroot kept on referring to as Original Thought. He drove me back home, we shot down the Relief Road at 100mph, and I screamed my lungs out. The floodlights were out at Windsor Castle – you could see the Round Tower and the ramparts in silhouette.

The next morning, he rang my house, he told my mum his

name was Schoolly D who is this rapper who makes songs about smoking cheeba cheeba all the time, and he asked me if I wanted to go out with him. I said yes of course, and that I'd see him after I'd finished a bit more work on the sketches of my Cerberus tattoo. This series is inspired by William Blake's Great Red Dragon paintings and I can't wait to show them to everybody.

Beetroot will be my first serious boyfriend; the thought of it all gave me a fizzy feeling in my legs and around my kidneys and bum hole.

Rowan | Next time, I'll be true…

I was over by the Stairway to Heaven waiting for Imogen after work, but nobody came down, so I inked-in some outlines in my sketch book. All the time I was there I could hear this tinny music playing in the distance. I climbed up to the top step, sometimes you can see where people have made hollows out in the crops, but I couldn't make all that much out as there was a wind making the wheat stalks sway in a dance. It must have been a tape player because I could hear the same song as it kept coming and going on the breeze. The one that goes, footsteps on the dance floor, remind me baby of you… It just went around and around, like the song does anyway – it seemed eternal and eerie. In fact, I felt a bit unnerved by the whole experience. Teardrops in my eyes, the next time I'll be true… At first, I thought it might have been Imogen because she really likes that one.

After about ten minutes of searching around in the field, I found a clearing in the wheat where the music was coming from. The wind kept on changing so its source was difficult to pinpoint at first. I lost my sense of direction and got turned around about twice, crisscrossing my old route. In the end though, I found where Womack & Womack were hiding.

In a small hollow, there was a fit looking guy fast asleep on a blanket next to a small tape player. He didn't respond when I said hello. After pushing him in the side with my foot I just stood watching him for a minute or so. I know it's a bit wacko, but I was reluctant to touch him again in case I startled him, but in the end, when I was sure he was out-of-it, I sat him up and dressed him in his top and then I pulled my hat onto his head as you lose most of your heat through your head. I didn't want him to die of the cold like Luca did. The Teardrops song carried on and it began to make me feel sad for Gene and how shit I'd been to Warren. Even though it's a fast song the lyrics are wistful, I think the woman is apologising to her ex-boyfriend for cheating on him, and that whatever happened had happened a long time ago – it's about regret. Sometimes, I want to take back all the awful things I've said or thought, the times when I didn't mean a lot of what I said or did, but we can't unsay things like that, we have to live with what we've done, you can't tie up every loose end; the people you've wronged won't always let you or allow you back inside to give you the needed closure – they think nursing a slight is more valuable to them than forgiveness. Gene might not have been the right person for me, but we could have still been friends and now he's gone. Warren, I hardly know, but I scared him off. He was just being loyal to his wife. How can I get upset at someone for doing right by their wife? If we were together then all it means is he wouldn't cheat on me – I mean if he wasn't already married to scarf lady. It shows he's good and not everybody is. I think when I see him next, I'll say I'm sorry, and ask if we can start again, just as friends. Then again, maybe I won't.

Anyway, I'm losing the thread of what I wanted to tell you; when I was in the field, I knew I had to act quickly so I ran to the phone box and called Hope whose mum works as a volunteer at the temporary hospital. She said she'd try and get somebody sent, so I went back to where I'd found the sleeper.

When Hope showed up, she was with that moron Beetroot, I asked if they were going out and they giggled and said yes. He said they were on their first date and gave me an ironic double thumbs up before ruffling Hope's hair up; I just shook my head and tutted at the patent lameness. Anyway, I showed them where the stranger was sleeping and Beetroot said, nice hat, when he saw him in my hat. I ignored him but he didn't get the message and carried on making thick comments regardless which Hope laughed at; she was clearly besotted by this birk. Beetroot's got a van, and Hope figured it would be better just to put him in there than to get a green ambulance over as it would take ages and they had planned to see a film together later that night. Apparently, they were showing a doggy double-bill at The Maybox of Lassie Come Home and 101 Dalmatians. I mean, those two going to watch kids' films? Personally, I thought it sounded like a crap night out but I didn't say as much – I didn't get invited anyway.

Mum's been away at Wembley Arena to a big dog convention all week called A Pause for Paws. Her and her friend Manuela were there to do a talk/lecture and run a stall to raise awareness for the Dog Necropolis in Slough and talk about the wildlife living there. She basically raises funds for its upkeep as it is a registered charity. Mum invites me to go to Wembley and Crufts with her every year, but I never go, not anymore. Not since I was a kid. It's too sad. It gets a grip on you; you can feel the death on your skin. I didn't know what the sensation was as a kid but it's easy to recognise now.

All the while we were moving the sleeper about, he didn't stir at all, he was just breathing in and out like anybody else would when they are fast asleep. I'd read about the sleepers and mates had told me about their encounters, but this was my first. Thinking about it, I guess Luca was one of the earliest, it's a good job this guy had his radio on loud as we wouldn't have found him. Maybe he planned it that way, but why play a tape? They only last half an hour/forty-five minutes or so each side, maybe it was a suicide attempt. But then there was no guarantee you'd actually remain asleep. I couldn't riddle it out.

I didn't go to the racecourse with Hope and Beetroot as I didn't want to get creeped out any more than I already was. They said it was OK, that I'd done my bit. I took my hat back off the sleeper, but I didn't put it on my head in case I caught whatever he had.

Astrid | Some grand design…

I got sent a video tape from my university today; it was from one of my future professors and it was an introduction to narrative assembly. They took coincidence as the basis of the lecture, and how there's no such thing as a real one in fiction because everything has been fabricated for the story. No matter how fleeting the coincidence is, it simply doesn't exist because it's all a construct of a single author's mind. The professor went on to say that no matter how deft the writer was, the story would never escape the cancerous contrivance at its centre. I've seen coincidences in real life, everybody has, and I don't know how they work. Like, I'll be humming an old song, and then I'll hear it on the radio a moment later, you know, there's no explanation for it. Or I'll think about somebody then run into them in the street at random as if I've summoned them. I've begun to write down the occurrences I can remember from over the course of my life and now I've filled a small notebook from cover to cover. Some are big, some are small, but what can you do with them? I guess you just have to acknowledge they've happened; you recognise them, point them out to friends or family and then move on. The professor said coincidences are evidence of a certain pattern, some grand design we're not privy to, and yet its architects stay shrouded. That it has everything to do with an unpopular school of thought in current quantum theory, called the Pavla Szerkovska Law which I couldn't follow but will look up and learn later. In essence, the lecturer thought there's no real way to know how or why coincidences occur and that numbers lie at the heart of the mechanism. And as I'm beginning a creative writing degree in a month's time, I can't write a story about them unless I really apply myself, but I don't know if I can incorporate one convincingly without being very obvious.

For our holiday, Synnøve and I are going to an island off the west coast of Sicily called Levanzo; some of her friends including Enos are coming along with us. We are staying at a tiny pensione, and we are looking forward to going for walks, swimming from the beaches, and getting ourselves a tan. Synnøve was telling me we can go scuba diving and see first-century vases on the seabed. Synnøve has packed a radio for us to play when we sunbathe so people can find us if we fall asleep and come and wake us up. Italy is in chaos because their hospitals are overrun but it's not been announced as a state of emergency yet. Synnøve said that after countries begin to declare this kind of status there's no turning back for them. I don't want to act scared, but I do get anxious. It's the same as being afraid of the dark, kind of. Dreading nightfall.

Rowan | As a species...

People's houses are getting burgled all the time and the police can't keep up. Mum said the army gets called-in in situations where the police force can't cope and that will be bad for everyone. I don't know anyone personally who's had their house broken into yet, but Eton Wick isn't exactly millionaire's row, it's places like Ascot, Sunningdale, Dorney, Taplow and bits of Windsor or Boulter's Lock in Maidenhead that have been getting hit according to the local rag. If anybody breaks into our house, there's nothing but photos of dogs to steal. Mum thinks the human race is going to end up extinct just like the dogs, but they never went to sleep like we're doing. Their exit was different and quick; pups, old dogs, every dog, all breeds, a rapid cough, choking, followed by a seizure then abracadabra, exodus. It's as if the very air they breathed had turned bad. Over the course of two weeks virtually every single dog on the planet was dead – there was a massive funeral pyre two storeys high on Bachelor's Acre in Windsor, various local farmers dug deep burial pits on their land. Mum told me about the plumes of black smoke seen rising from farmland all across the Thames

Valley. Not everybody could afford to inter their dogs in the pet cemeteries that were set up in the wake of the deaths. Many people buried their dogs at home or in the wilds. We heard international news stories where some dogs were saved for a while, preserved on special ventilators, frozen, but nothing held, it was all temporary; even the richest of the rich couldn't save man's best friend. They think a novel pathogen took them, something in the atmosphere changed or some malevolent spores were unleashed, a weaponised fungi or pollen, but they still don't know. Whenever the scientific community comes close to putting all the pieces together, the missing piece would contradict everything they surmised forcing them to rethink everything again from another angle, only to be scuppered in the same way with a different jigsaw piece. That's how it's been told to me again and again. Everybody knows the dogs aren't with us anymore, and we all have our theories only we don't talk about it anymore, do we? The people who go to Crufts like Mum are viewed as cranks on the margins of society. I think it's the shame we feel, a kind of disgust with ourselves, and at our leaders for offering us no resolution, no closure – that nobody or any one thing has been held accountable. It's a failing on massive scale. But we look away, we don't want to shoulder the blame, or live with the knowledge that their extinction was our fault. Mum says it's because we're the only ones with the ability to talk about it, yet as a species, we've chosen not to, and that cats, birds, snakes, weasels and the rabbits also noticed the dogs were gone but they have no words, so it's as if us humans have followed suit – we've held our tongues and fallen in line with all the other animals. As a species, we're a haunted house inhabited by phantasmagorical dogs.

Some thought the death of dog-kind was an omen, that humans were living off a borrowed dollar, but then no one is talking sense. If you read the newspapers and watch the TV all the time you'll drown, but on the other hand if you don't get the facts from official sources, then you only get to hear rumours, anti-information, and conspiracy theories people have just thought up on the bus or walking out in the crops – everybody has their theory, everybody wants to be heard, yet nobody is original – nothing is picked up through personal observation, it's all just arrived at through exposure to TV and the papers and around it all goes. Yet no one talks about the dogs, they can't hack it, it's like everybody has forgotten, or are ignoring it because they know we might be next. They ignore all the sleeping birds, the pets and the farm animals in the fields we drive past every day on the way to work. It's not just us sliding away into sleep.

I was in the woods down near the Thames Path, by Dorney Church last Sunday for a wander and there was no birdsong, just the creaking of timber. I found an old nest that had crashed to the ground at some point but there was no sign of any birds.

Gene | A real man's love…

Playing records with Bob and Boodlal at The Trout on Thursday, it was much busier than expected. As we played Tougher Than the Rest by Bruce Springsteen (a real man's love song – ha ha) this skinny guy in dungarees looking like a young Errol Brown from Hot Chocolate, moustache and all, came up to me and said, I hear you're looking for Slave. I was a bit put out he knew this, but Bob smiled at the guy and said, hello Roger, Gene this is Roger. For a second things were a bit tense, but this guy smiled a lot and was pretty funny, so I let my guard down a bit – I don't like strange people knowing my business or what I'm about, not that I've got anything to hide, I don't know what it is. As Bob packed his records away at the end, he explained that Roger was a graff writer and he reckoned he had recently seen Slave finishing off one of his dog murals at The Pit. He said everybody at the Slough writers' bench was trying to work out who he was, and they knew absolutely everyone for miles, toys included, whether they concentrated on buildings or trains. Me and Bob stayed away from the bench but even we were known. They left us alone because we were down with Red Shoes FM and we made sure never to go over anybody else's pieces. The bench had deduced that Slave was this rudeboy called Manfred Bennings who lived in Chalvey. Roger said he'd spotted him at The Pit but hadn't followed him because he didn't want to give up his position. Then he went on to say he thought Manfred lived in this three-storey house on the corner of Ledgers Road and Chalvey High Street by the railway bridge which was some kind of halfway house for people who had been in borstal or young offenders. Manfred worked on Saturdays in a clothes shop on Farnham Road just down from Slough Record Centre. There's a good spray can shop up there, car maintenance and stuff, Roger and Bob said we should all go up there and suss him out a bit.

I saw Rowan in town earlier the same night, she was with Imogen and Astrid and a few others. They didn't see me – they were sitting outside the front door of The Donkey House drinking pints of cider, and I was leaning on the railings overlooking the river towards Eton. I was telling my older mate Greg Fraser about Manjit, and he shared with me the fact that quite a few people in the office where he worked had been signed off because they had become sleepers. Also, that half of his colleagues were new temps.

Rowan looked good, and she was laughing with Astrid and Imogen. After a bit, Leon Deeley and his buddy David Tee turned up and they all went off somewhere else together. Greg said he was feeling tired, but he bought a Lucozade from Londis on our way over to The Trout. He went home after another pint – he said he couldn't stop yawning but he enjoyed the tunes Bob and Boodlal were playing. I couldn't agree, as they played Push It by Salt-n-Pepa which is well shit; I'm sure they play that tune to wind me up.

I'd brought along some records to play; one was by a new group called Caveman, this track called Victory – they are from High Wycombe and that's just up the road, sort of.

The Chorus | Perhaps you were born…

Where were you when the dogs left? Do you remember? How long ago was 1975? Was it one year ago, two, ten years, longer?

Have you even seen a dog? Perhaps you were born after 1975, perhaps you've only seen dogs in photographs, in old films.

Do you remember the failed attempts to splice dog DNA with that of a wolf? Do you remember the series of experiments when scientists and dog-trainers attempted to domesticate wolves? How the wolves couldn't be trained; they bored quickly of human company – food wasn't enough to keep them in our thrall. We'll never bond with wolves because they don't look us in the eye. We distrust them because they know things we don't and they just don't like us – and I don't blame them, look what we did to the dogs, our dearest and best. Domestic wolves which are treated in the same fashion as dogs tend to become depressed and prone to developing anti-social behaviours. Wolves should never be made subservient as it runs counter to their natural instincts. They are of the wilderness, they never wanted to come across to us; enforcing our domestic wiles on them can lead to harm and animal trauma and the annihilation of their very essence.

All the experiments came to no good end anyway. Hundreds of wolves were put down, scientists discredited, and hearts everywhere remained broken because of our meddling.

Have you ever been to Crufts? Have you been to Crufts since the dogs left us behind? Do you pretend your dog is still alive like so many former dog owners do? Is the dog's lead still hung up by the front door, or is it raveled up in your old winter coat pocket? In the back of the kitchen cupboard, is there still a stash of Pedigree Chum hiding in there? Do you pay a man or woman to be your surrogate dog, your cuddle pet? Do they come to your house when your husband/wife/partner is out? Do you fall asleep in their paws? Have you ever bought any of those cans of dog scent? Do you spray your outdoor coat with the contents or smear scent residue on your pillow at night to entice your dead dogs to visit you in your dreams?

The Chorus | Such was the dog

Do you think people are lonelier now? I think they probably are. Such was the dog, you could strike up a conversation with anybody. A kindly comment to another dog owner or the enjoyment of some admiration for your dog from a passer-by was commonplace. After they left us, we became marooned... the tide rose yet again to cut us off to make us even more like islands. Another avenue of casual access to our fellow humans was lost to us – parks became ever more dangerous afterwards.

Don't forget how much closer we all were back then, that's been lost forever now. When we were young, we never used to look in the mirror. Now it's all the young have left – they don't even have any canine memories to lose.

Astrid | Men that I trust...

This morning after breakfast, in my new notebook, I wrote a list of all the men that I trust and all the men I don't.

I trust two men and I don't even know one of them very well. One of them is Lance, and I suppose that's obvious, but I also have a good feeling about Synnøve's friend Enos too. I feel like he's a good person, but I can't decide why yet, I hardly know him, but I get a hopeful feeling.

On the list of men I don't trust is Crap Craig, he's in pole position. He still hasn't apologised to Mum or acknowledged what he did to Synnøve a few weeks ago. Every time Mum has brought the subject up with him, he has shouted her down, or marched out the front door. Last time it got really heated and he smashed a dinner plate and stamped a boiled potato into the carpet. I asked her why she doesn't break up with him, and she said he owed her a little bit of money. That's a rubbish reason to keep someone around, as a hundred pounds isn't all that much money.

I don't trust any of the men and boys at work. Ash is short-sighted and self-serving; he never protects us from trouble like abusive customers. He just wants us to work fast and shut up.

I don't trust Gene because he doesn't have spatial awareness. He stands too close to you, and he doesn't mind touching you when he walks past; he's not grabby but he gets really close, and he smells of Bovril. I don't think his mum lets his clothes dry properly because they have that chewy cheese pong all the time plus he uses too much hair gel that gives him spots along the bottom of his fringe. He would probably be OK if he didn't smell so much and resisted this urge he has to belch and fart in front of everybody all the time.

Beetroot is a late yet high entry on the list. He is lazy and I know he's always watching me. I also know I'm in that shitty book of his too. Hope said Schrodinger's List doesn't even exist, it's just in his head, I don't know why she's lying because I've seen the book and I know she has too. The Schrodinger thing is a stupid joke anyway; are you on the list or aren't you, you'll never know (ha ha) unless you look inside and until then you won't know. He's so irritating and disgusting.

I still don't know what Hope sees in Beetroot, but I guess it's because she's younger than us/him, she likes the attention…it's still new – it's always amazing with your first few guys I suppose. Ash told Beetroot to put her down as he saw him feeling Hope up on the shop floor. He has double standards though because I saw him stroking Casey's face when they were talking in the magazine aisle. For the last week it's become obvious they are a thing now. Neither him nor Casey have talked to any of us about their relationship, it's as if they think they are a cut above us and we don't count. I can't wait to leave that place behind.

I don't trust the old men at the pub either. The ones who watch me as I walk home, I can feel their eyes on me, it's as if they look out for me especially. They never say anything, they just stand around staring, holding their pints around the doorway, nudging each other, winking over their saggy bellies, peering over the top of their spectacles, multiple chins and long noses at me. They think I don't notice what they're doing, I think a lot of men like that are programmed to leer as standard, they can't help it.

I don't trust my Dad, Birgo, and that's even if he is still alive. He hasn't been in contact with any of us for over fifteen years – he vanished from family life around the same time the dogs faded away – he didn't follow us to England. Mum is certain he is dead; according to her, he had turned into some penniless alcoholic barfly back in Oslo; nobody back there had seen him in over a decade. He'd been living in a flophouse near Vigeland Park and this big cinema with a domed roof I remember from when I was a kid. Maybe one day, I'll try to pick up his trail, until then he's just this question mark. I don't think about him every day or even every week, in fact, I almost forgot to add him to this list.

The Chorus | Only asleep for a day...

Today, some of the newspapers including the broadsheets are running a story reporting that an estimated one and half million people in the UK alone have succumbed to long-term sleep or what they are now referring to as an FND, which stands for functional neurological disorder in case you weren't aware – I don't how much you already know, sorry. So far, only five thousand or so have woken up again. Of those who came back, a high proportion were only asleep for a couple of days, whilst a much smaller number were out-of-it for as long as two weeks. I don't know if it's going to get better or worse, nobody does. Everybody's being strangely quiet about it all at home, in the workplace, at the clubhouse and this eerie reluctance to speak extends to the government and the popular media at large.

Rowan | I can't stop wondering…

Some of the lads at Daniels have signed up to join the Territorial Army and have been accepted right away as if on some whim. They are to be stationed at Combermere Barracks in Windsor for a bit before going down to Aldershot or Salisbury Plain for further induction. I guess that's where they get turned from boys to men. I saw my friends Leon and David at The Donkey House a few nights ago and they said they are going to be part of a peacekeeping troop that will probably be deployed in cities and towns to help the police. Leon told us the pay is way better than at Daniels, and he'll most probably stay on after the trouble dies down if he likes it. Leon's clean-living and pretty buff already from all the sports he plays – rowing, rugby, blah; he's got this powerful motorbike and a hot and shiny new Toyota Corolla too, so a lot of the pretty girls adore him. He lives up St Leonard's Hill in a big, gated house, his family are loaded. He had planned to go to university in Brighton after the summer, but now he's deferred entry just to help out. Leon was born and raised in Singapore and has lived over here for about 5 years now. For a rich kid, he's alright – he's not too much of a Flash Harry.

That was the same night I saw Gene. He was standing by the river talking to an older guy with a beard who I didn't recognise at all. I knew Gene had seen me because he was facing in our direction, but he never came over. He was wearing that same green overcoat, and black Champion sweater like he always does. After a while he turned his back on us and leant on the railings, drinking with his friend. Seeing him there brought it all back to me, it helped me see that the past is the past. He seems happy to let me carry on without him, I should do the same. I can't stop wondering about how he is though. I miss being around him even though he's a total pig. I don't know which feels worse, being with him or longing for him. If this is what love is, then it's broken.

Hope | Same for him…

One of our friends from the village, Imogen, has been taken to the racecourse. I asked Mum if she could find out whereabouts in the hospital she was sleeping. As soon as she let us know on the phone me and Beetroot drove over.

The roads from Eton Wick make a weird figure of eight shape between my house and the racecourse. You see the road from Eton Wick fly under the Relief Road about five minutes after you drive over the top of it and down into Windsor.

Once we had parked up at the racecourse, we could see about a hundred, I'm not joking, sleepers out in the sun, all sitting in wheelchairs or lying on gurneys. At first, I couldn't work out what I was hearing – it sounded like cats purring, but I discovered it was all the sleepers gently snoring as I got closer. I thought they would be in danger of getting sunburnt to be honest but I'm sure someone had their eyes on them all.

Mum met us at reception, I could see her sizing Beetroot up right away, and she just came out with it, I don't want him sleeping over. You should have asked. Then she told him to wait at the entrance for us as she wanted to talk to me. She said she hoped I was taking precautions, that this wasn't the right time to have kids full-stop what with everyone nodding off (her words, not mine), that anybody getting pregnant in a pandemic needed their fucking selfish heads testing. I even haven't gone all the way with Beetroot yet, so why is she misjudging me like this? She never gives me any credit.

Mum has this saying she wheels out at every relevant opportunity that promiscuous animals have small brains. It never fails to make me laugh no matter how serious she's being. It always makes me flashback to a visit to Windsor Safari Park with my nan when I was small. We were at the monkey enclosure watching these macaques all sitting in a row along a massive rope span and they were wriggling and all cuddled in close front-to-back. There were some older boys on the viewing platform, and I recall them pointing and laughing – all of a sudden, their mum smacked their bare legs for being typical dirty boys. It took a minute for the penny to drop with my nan that the monkeys were actually bumming each other, so she took me by the hand and led me away explaining they were just bouncing up and down to keep flies off their fur.

Mum doesn't know shit about shit anyway because I made Beetroot sleep in the living room; he still came into my bed in the middle of the night saying he'd gotten lonely. We didn't make out or anything; I was knackered and it was far too hot; his thick old erection was poking me in the arse all night – in the end I kicked him out for being a pest.

Imogen looked very peaceful. Even though she's a sleeper, she knows it's daytime, a passing nurse announced to us. I must have been showing something she could read on my face, but I can't work out how my expressions look from inside.

The only signs Imogen wasn't taking a simple nap was the tube coming out of her nose, the plaster on her cheek. I crouched down and said hello and kissed her on the cheek. I hoped she could recognise my voice, but I told her it was me anyway, and immediately felt like very self-concious.

I'm not looking forward to having to go to my caring classes which are starting in two days. I've told Ash he has to change my shift around, but he hasn't yet. If he doesn't, I'm just going to go anyway, because it's a government requirement that I attend. Beetroot said he'd cover my shift because we're not working on the same days – a swap would be a cinch. Mum was saying they are only accepting sleepers at the racecourse who have nobody else at home to care for them as of next Monday. It's sad, what if your whole family is asleep and you're the last one?

Mum came back after a while with a nurse who took Imogen's blood pressure which was 120/81, which is normal she told us – it meant nothing to me. I was beginning to think about Beetroot waiting out front when Mum began to move Imogen's limbs, bending and stretching her knees, joints and elbows, rolling her hips and wrists. As Mum prepared to wash her, I kissed Imogen again and left.

Beetroot said his first caring class was the week after I had mine. Our local caring classes were taking place in the hall attached to the side of the big church where Luca's funeral was. Everyone between fifteen and twenty-five was being rounded up first to learn some basic routines and things which could help a sleeper in your family, like bed baths, taking pulses and blood pressure, oxygen feeds, exercises and loads of stuff. I suppose you have the same courses where you are. Everyone around here had two classes, then they were on their own. Beetroot went on to say he thought he'd be shit at caring for his family if they became sleepers, but he knew they'd do the same for him if he succumbed. I assured him it all looked quite easy because I'd just seen Imogen get some light physiotherapy and the beginnings of a bed bath. Beetroot wants to stay working for as long as he can, right until the end. I told him there wouldn't be an ending, that the worst won't happen, it never does, and we'll carry on like we always do. But then he said, what about the dogs?

The Chorus | Speak to say nothing…

We only ever had one dog when I was growing up. It was this big, raggedy-arsed thing called Lassie. The thing was wild, big shaggy coat, and it stank to high heaven, I tell ya. Me da had brought it back with him from the pub one day, he couldn't say no to nothing, me da – right soft touch he was. Stern but soft.

One day, we was down Jubilee Park and it shot off after this old fella on a bike, out through the gates and down Dinas Lane past Alan's Chinese towards Huyton Village. We couldn't find her anywhere. We were bereft, we looked all over the place for her, for days we looked. We drew pictures of her and had them stuck in shop windows, lamp posts, you know. But we heard nothing. She was gone. Us kids were dead upset, crying our eyes out we were.

Then, I don't know, two, three weeks go by, and we see this fella's walking Lassie in the park where we lost her, me and my sisters were thrilled to see her. The man was puzzled as to how we knew his dog. We tried to tell him the dog was ours, but he wasn't having it. He wasn't shitty or nothing, he just told us kids to calm down and he'd come and have a word with our dad if we showed him where we lived. Us kids pretty much escorted him around our house to see Da like he was under an armed guard or something.

We watched them talk for a bit, me Da and the man, out past the garden gate in the close and saw them shake hands, the stranger handed Lassie's lead over to him. And that's that. Not sure what happened you know. Me da, he didn't speak to say nothing, he was a quiet man – he just told us to keep a firm grip on the animal next time we all went out. Can't remember what happened to that dog. I'll have to ask our Margie when I see her next, she remembers everything, even being born, her memory's that good. She has this saying I like. It goes, memories are all the butterfly has left of the caterpillar, she's very Zen like that, our kid.

The Chorus | Tidal de-spin

Mare Humboldtianum

Aitken

Mare Australe

Oresme

Mare Frigoris

Berkner

Mare Ingenii

Pettitt

Mare Orientale

Cantor

Mare Moscoviense

Oppenheimer

Tianjin

Izsak

Jenner

Vallis Bouvard

Vallis Inghirami

The Chorus | Bad things in faraway places

You have one life on Earth, use it up, the orator on the Bible course I've been sending off for says, and I know what she means; some evenings I feel it too, but we don't talk like that at all in my house. Instead, we talk about our day at work, we talk about the things we need to put on our to-do lists, we say things we may regret later.

We mainly talk to one another at mealtimes; we talk about not eating meat, we talk about the film we watched on the television last night, we talk about the plight of starving Africans, we talk about the demolition of the Berlin Wall and the upcoming reunification of Germany, the IRA attacks in London and on MPs, the Iraqi invasion of Kuwait, the independence of Namibia, we talk about Jesus and his disciples, the Hubble telescope, the bloody Poll Tax, FW de Klerk and Apartheid, we talk about the new decade, we talk about Michael Jackson, and also of bad things happening in faraway places like Libya, Sri Lanka, Burma, Nicaragua, Chechnya, and Israel. We sing along to our Rattle and Hum tape in the kitchen.

We tell each other stories about humans, yet we don't talk about our humanity. We certainly don't talk about the absence of dogs, we don't talk about their lives, their abilities, their astonishing olfactory senses, their abilities to detect illness and disease in humans. In bed at night, the astonishing yet abnormal moonlight troubles us, it makes us ask ourselves questions like this: is God punishing us? Is He punishing me? Does He forgive what I did to Petronius? Do the others know? Did my dog love me as much as I loved him? Did Petronius know we were kind, that other dogs live in suffering? Will he seek me out when it's my turn to enter through the gates of Heaven? Will he be able to pick up my scent? Will he recognise it; will he come and find me in the crowds pushing his snout through the forest-like legs of the saved?

We don't talk about dogs because we know what we've done. And now we're really not talking about our own imminent ending on Earth – how it may go for all of us one day. We really aren't. In these testing times, I lean into Jesus and I pray to God. In the church on Sunday, there is a new strain of silence. Father Dsane doesn't want to talk about it with us. Perhaps he's had a crisis of faith – attendance has dwindled dramatically – he asked us in earnest if we had to believe in God to lead a religious life. None of us had the answer. We just had questions, the same as he did. How many are sleepers, how many are lost sheep – do they even amount to the same thing? How long until we'd all be asleep and what's the difference between a lost sleeper and a saved one? Our provincial holy men are leading us into the void.

The Chorus | Our beds are catafalques

The first I knew that the dogs were in dire trouble was back when I was living just outside Bideford in Devon back in 1975. I was walking on the path above the shoreline, downriver on the Torridge towards Appledore; my dog Cinders was walking at heel carrying her lead in her mouth like she so often did. I spotted a woman I vaguely knew to say hello to with her terrier – they were out on a wooden boardwalk used for accessing small launches at low tide – this is where I saw them most mornings. Me and Cinders stopped to watch them, I gave the woman a wave and she responded in turn. Her little dog barked to mark our arrival; I can see it in my mind's eye as it ran along the boardwalk – it was a scruffy little thing with a chequered bowtie. When it reached the woman, it stopped, looked down at its front paws then began to cough. Again and again it coughed, then a few times more – each time it shook its head vigorously. We saw the woman reach down to pat the dog on the stomach. I noticed Cinders was watching intently studying the scene, her ears were up, her eyes fixed on the stricken dog. The dog continued to cough like it was choking on something caught in its throat. Within seconds the woman had picked her dog up, nursing it as it coughed a few more times, then its body seemed to go limp in her arms. With this she began to run urgently along the boardwalk. Cinders and I observed them until they disappeared behind a row of house boats and then some nearby fishermen's shacks.

As we headed for home, Cinders kept on looking back at the boardwalk to where the small dog had been for a long time afterwards, periodically rooting her feet to the ground. It's as if she had an inkling of what was coming for her. For all of us.

Death gives us no sign of its arrival, it's as if it's been here all along – our beds are merely catafalques in waiting.

The Chorus | Our own disappearance...

The mirrors inveigle the seasons through the room, even their shadows; the windows in my house are only small.

The world without any dogs, to me, became unfamiliar quickly – it had transformed into a world without innocence. The destruction of the dogs was the death of infinite possibility. Now, I feel like we're all waiting for our own disappearance but I'm not afraid.

The Chorus | Note their existence…

We can recognise events as coincidences and yet what of them? We note their existence and carry on, they don't change anything, we can't change them, their patterns cannot be traced or predicted. It's just the way events turn from time-to-time, and we must accept this; there is no higher power at work. The pathway winds on into the darkness. Answers don't exist where we're going – if they ever did exist then they have fallen into the gaps, down into those mysterious dark fissures where sense and logic vanish off to. I sit and wonder if there was ever any more to us than our mistakes.

The Chorus | Don't take our cats...

Have you seen those greeting cards saying, 'Dog is God spelt backwards?' What does it mean? Are they trying to tell us God has left us too? People are past understanding.

Some think a simple prayer is the fix. We're so sorry God, we'll do better. Please give us back our dogs, don't take our cats. But I don't believe in God anymore, I've stopped – then, he doesn't believe in me either.

The Chorus | Past the atmospheric seal…

All I hear is the dog statue howling from its hillside in Slough – I wonder what type of person feels the need to reach out to press that button. As the howls ripple out into outer space up beyond the cloud canopy, past the atmospheric seal, just like every other broadcast we've ever made, do you think the cascading souls of our pets hurtling through the void for the past fifteen years will hear them? Will they see they've been remembered and that we're sorry for what happened?

The person pressing the button/sending the message mutters the words, I'm still here, again and again under their breath.

The button on the dog monument's side panel glows electric blue as it howls – then it turns red when the noise begins to abate.

The Chorus | Why you broke away…

Isn't home the place where we all begin and return to? Don't we go back home to achieve a sense of self-realisation – to get ourselves put back together again? It's a risky business returning to the scene of a crime.

Most of the time we return only to discover that we're no more advanced or enriched having gone away. You find that your friends and family are falling over themselves to tell you about all the good stuff you missed while you were far away yet all it takes is a few days, just a few, to rediscover the reasons why you broke away in the first place. You absorb the boredom, observe the dynamics of old relationships replaying themselves – all the history repeating itself. You rub your eyes in dismay as kids you used to know peer back at you from their lined and lumpy forty/fifty-year old faces. You were the one that left, they stayed and got aged, had kids – what's the real thing that separates you from them though? Did you miss out on more of the grimy stuff of life, perhaps you lost out on more love, more involvement, more trauma through being absent. Is it really true they're the ones who've led unfulfilled lives though? You keep telling yourself this lie and it rings false but you keep this knowledge hidden inside. All that truly remains come drawdown are the choices you ignored and the chances you took – it doesn't really matter where you were, surrounded by the people you grew up with or new ones you collected on your travels. There's a weird power in not being there but perhaps everybody forgot about you the minute you climbed aboard the bus out, maybe they were glad you went; you probably made them all restless and uneasy, especially the wise ones who've always known there's nothing out there for you or anybody else. Sky, land covered with buildings, jungles, deserts, rivers, mountains, hill ranges, gorges, valleys, roads, animals, fish, birds, insects, reptiles, fungi, cells, other people, the bottom of the deep blue sea, the living, the dead, the same mysteries, infinity, nothing. An arrival close to a conclusion that there's really nothing out there and worst still there's nothing in here either, inside with us.

The Chorus | East but less…

I cast my memory clearly on down to that early morning in Berlin when I saw an old lady attacking her dog with a stick.

Back in the late sixties, I was a sales rep for a leather company. I'd had breakfast at my hotel and decided to take a stroll around the city. Back then, of course, the city was subdivided yet I had visas to pass between East and West Berlin. My case of samples would come under a lot of scrutiny in the east but less so on the western side, yet beyond the checkpoints my days in Berlin were relatively humdrum. I always left myself a lot of time to make journeys across the city; queues reared their head at unusual times in peculiar locations; busy periods at the border check points seemed utterly random.

On the morning I want to tell you all about, I was walking in the Tiergarten close to Siegaussäule when I happened upon the cruel scene. The aggrieved dog was standing on three paws with its front right paw up as if to curry favour with its owner. But the woman was incensed, every few seconds she lashed out at the dog with her tree branch but at each turn it slowly outmanoeuvred her swipes. On the fifth or sixth attempt she struck the dog and it yelped and rolled over onto its back in submission, its ears down – only the woman raised her stick again and I thought she was going to do the dog some serious injury. This was when I called out to her – I commanded her to stop, and she froze. I asked her what she thought she was doing. Was it her own dog she was attacking, or had it been bothering her before I appeared? She replied in halting German that it was her dog, and she could do whatever she liked. I went towards her and took the stick from her and threw it into the undergrowth. This was when her dog got to its feet and began to growl at me, it positioned itself between myself and the woman, baring its teeth at me. You leave us alone – this is none of your business, warned the woman. She will bite you if I use her trigger word you know. She will tear your intestines out. With that the dog began to bark angrily without advancing on me. She will protect me, the woman added. Protect me against men like you. I walked away – there wasn't a lot I could do. As I reached the bend in the parkway, I looked back and I saw this peculiar dog owner patting her dog on the head then attaching a lead to its collar. Best friends again.

I'm not a dog expert, who is? But all I'm sure of is this. It was her dog, and as cruel as she was, her pet would have defended her against me at the expense of its own well-being.

The Chorus | Sixteen on the premises...

I know where I was on the day the dogs began to die in 1975. It was back when I had that converted water tower. A unique old place situated within a hundred metres of the English Channel at Littlestone-on-Sea. I'll never forget it.

On the morning of that day, I awoke to find sixteen dogs in my basement. I had no idea where they'd come from. It took me a long time to work out how they'd got inside and where the heck they'd come from.

I lived alone at the time and on the majority of mornings I was conned out of my sleep by the screech of seagulls. This morning, however, their familiar shrieks had been replaced by dog barks.

Downstairs in the kitchen the noise of the dogs was hellish. There was scratching and bashing as the latch on the trapdoor in the kitchen floor rattled and the wooden door itself boomed and shook. Instead of opening the door, I phoned my friend, Bronagh from Dungeness, to ask what I should do.

From out of my bedroom window, I remember looking out across my garden to the beach and the sea beyond, all looked as it should. Order, calm, and order again. The dogs yowled and carried on from below the trapdoor.

On investigation outside, the double doors to the cellar from the garden side of the tower were swinging open in the onshore winds. The chain which once firmly wrapped the big wooden panel fence-like doors about their handles was nearby, mysteriously coiled on the gravel driveway like a giant sleeping adder. A little while later, I noticed a gun dog on the lawn sniffing around a bush. I tried to shoo it away, but it ignored me. Once I'd caught hold of the hound about its collar, I read its name tag. The hound's name was Brown – there was also a phone number on it.

When my friend Bronagh pulled up in her car a short while later, we went down into the basement to see how many other dogs were around including Brown, and as I stated earlier, there were sixteen on the premises. Most of them were very much at ease by now and were sitting down, their bellies on the ground, supine. Some had collars, others didn't. Two of them were scrabbling at the trapdoor trying to get out but they seemed to relax somewhat when they saw us. One of the dogs leapt up and laddered my stockings with its dewclaws which made me cross as they were brand new. We rang some of the phone numbers to reach their owners, a number of whom were surprised and hadn't even noticed that their dogs had escaped or gone missing. By lunchtime, a man had come to collect his dog, only it had died by the time he showed up. It was a Labrador called Dreamer, and he was understandably confused and very upset, especially when we noticed three other dogs, including Brown, had also passed away. My first thought was that they'd eaten rat poison, so in the chaos we got all the dogs out of the basement – my second thought was that whoever had put all the dogs in the basement had poisoned them. Dreamer's owner called the police, and that's when we heard what was happening everywhere. We were told to switch the TV on and watch the breaking news.

All of the dog's owners were traced, eleven out of the sixteen dogs were still alive by the time the evening rolled around. All the pets had been claimed and removed whether they had lived or the opposite by teatime.

The sixteen weren't the last dogs I ever saw, but this was certainly the last time I ever touched a dog, stroked one, let one lick my hand, my cheek.

Astrid | Mountainous and dry...

Synnøve hired a driver in Palermo to take us out west to Trapani; the motorways were empty compared to the ones in England – it felt strange. We drove through so many tunnels and the countryside looked very mountainous and dry, yet the stubborn road never rose nor fell – stretches of our course sat upon unfeasibly tall plinths of concrete – the sky was a blue forge.

As the north coast spun by, I tried to translate the journey into prose like an author's words, scribbling down everything in my notepad as I saw it – I desperately need to work on my style; it is fun finding different ways to describe the everyday scenes we see (not that I come to Sicily every day – ha ha), I wish I was as articulate in person as I am on paper, but I guess that will come with age and experience.

I was excited to get to Trapani, where we caught the boat for Levanzo. First of all, we had a late lunch and a drink with Enos and his 'girlfriendy' mate Beatrice, who is Sicilian, in this coastal town which seemed to defy gravity. Its streets and buildings seemed to be carved into immensely high cliffs – there were boardwalks high above the sea and hundreds of homes with terracotta tile roofs and amber and cream stone walls that only birds could have reached – what was that place called? It was either Trabia or Cefalù, maybe.

In Sicily, Beatrice's name is pronounced Be-arr-tree-shay, and not how we say it, Beertriss. She taught us this over lunch, how to say it properly. Enos was surprised as he had known her for years I think, and it was the first time she told him how to say her name the right way. Beatrice is from a place called Marsala, which was about twenty miles down the coast from Trapani. **After we had lunch**, we drove there and we took an early evening walk around the town, which is beautiful, with all its tall buildings with corniced balconies and shuttered windows, and handsome boys on scooters; everyone seemed to have style there. I caught our reflections as we walked up to a shop window, and we looked cool too, how strange it felt to be surprised by your own appearance and feel good about it – I usually feel the opposite. Beatrice assured us we would love Levanzo, that there was nothing to do there but relax and enjoy the sunshine, read, drink, sleep, and make romance. We had all planned to come back to Trapani for more sightseeing around the town before we went back to the airport, but things never worked out that way in the end.

Levanzo was a short boat ride away and I was delighted because our quaint pensione overlooked the harbour. Enos and Beatrice stayed at a different one a few yards away from mine and Synnøve's. If you've ever been to Levanzo, you will already know that most of the buildings on the island cluster around the cove and there is a handful of bars, restaurants, and maybe two shops: it's all very charming – armies of cats.

167 | Cerberus

I think Beatrice and Enos are a couple, although Synnøve told me they had separate rooms at their pensione. They touch each other with ease, it looks easy, but I can't bring myself to run my hands across somebody, give my hands over to them the way they do, not even a light embrace – not even with Lance, in public, I don't want to be touched all the time. It feels heavy on me – but I suppose, as they are dancers, they give more of themselves up to each other, physically, without stipends – I understand.

Over the course of the week, I didn't get to talk to Enos all that much by himself, he was always with the three of us. But I did like the way he included everybody in the conversations, and he would ask my opinion on things. They mainly talked about dancers and the ballet; I've heard a few of the names before like Nureyev, Martha Graham, and Eric Hawkins but most of the time I hadn't. Enos carries around a small book of 20th century art in the pocket of his linen jacket and likes to share his favourite paintings with us – I've jotted the names of Willem de Kooning, Bridget Riley, Lucien Freud, David Hockney, Giorgio Morandi, Alan Davie, Paula Rego, and Avigdor Arikha to look up when I'm back home. He paraphrased this beautiful passage from a novel he's reading by Paul Bowles called The Sheltering Sky, it talks about life's great illusion, of how time appears to be infinite and about the small number of occasions you may replay a favourite childhood memory or see a full moon. How it all seems limitless whereas in fact it's not, we may only experience certain things a few times more. Do we know how many times we'll see a dolphin, or eat honeyed crumpets, have sex with someone we truly love, swim in a warm sea? Life is not an infinite well, yet it seems so.

It's so refreshing for me to be around people who aren't backstabbing each other or gossiping. People only do that when they have nothing interesting to occupy their minds – they turn on themselves and on each other, I think. It's really nice to learn about the art world and to ameliorate and refine my tastes. I've also been jotting down the names of films like Umberto D, Identification of a Woman, Solaris, Paris Texas, The Year My Voice Broke, The Painted Desert, Blue Velvet, The Cook The Thief The Wife and Her Lover, The Tin Drum, Red Desert, The Conversation, A Bande à Part, and pieces of music they talk about, Mahler, Vaughan Williams, Shostakovich, Arvo Pärt, John Cage. Actually, I'm a bit embarrassed about the films I like but I only ever really go and see Saturday night films at The Maybox with Imogen or Lance – the last things I saw were Pretty Woman and The Tall Guy. They say they like those films too, but I feel like they are making a detour in their bonhomie just to make me feel comfortable which is OK, but I hate being humoured. But I genuinely enjoy listening to them all converse about the things that inspire them. I think university will be a place where I can develop my tastes and find out for myself if I like films like Paris Texas, or painters like Keith Haring and David Hockney – to have a sensible opinion about theatres, dancing and acting techniques and all the rest. It's going to help me become the writer I want to be one day or even the mother or sister, wife. Levanzo was a social adventure, I was so thrilled, even, to eat pasta con le sarde with Marsala wine, or try completely unknown dishes like pasta alla norma, stigghiola, scacciata, or maccu soup. I felt like our little group was in a different world floating off the edge of my normal one, one in which I'd never have to see Crap

Craig, or the people at Eton Wick Services ever again. All this newness made me want to dive into the sea, swim down to the seabed through the blue and then burst back through the surface to embrace my life renewed. I felt so happy, but I couldn't show it completely, I wanted to make a good impression on Enos and Beatrice, to be a person my sister was proud of and to just be true to the person that I am becoming. And then I thought of Lance for the first time that day. How far I felt from him. I wondered what he was up to. Whether he was out with Beetroot and the Car Freaks, or just at home playing records or watching a video he'd rented from Film Galaxy – I answered a phone call at his place when I was at his flat and it was the video shop saying they had reserved a copy of Shocker for him, so he's probably enjoying a quiet one watching that with a pizza from Mona's. At that point, I really wanted to speak to him, but we'd agreed I probably wouldn't phone him as it would be very expensive. Instead, I made a mental note to send him a postcard, but I forgot all about him until our last day in Sicily.

The first evening we were there, our dinner was very late because the son of the owner of the restaurant had become a sleeper (that same day). This had left the restaurant understaffed because his wife was away in Trapani caring for her mother who had also succumbed to the sleeping disease sometime earlier. The owner, Carlo, apologized he hadn't found enough help and that tomorrow was a better day. We felt guilty as he must have been worried for his son and instead, he was in his kitchen cooking for us. Beatrice translated for us, but he did speak a little English. Italian is such a lovely language to listen to; I'd like to learn it one day.

On our second day, we plastered ourselves in mosquito repellent and suntan lotion and began to walk to the derelict lighthouse at the far end of the island. There is just one road on Levanzo and it snakes around the bay in both directions from the main village. To the west the road takes you to a very craggy beach with red and black rocks, and the other way it winds off around the coast, then after a while it disappears up into the wild interior of the island, high up above the harbour before it gets too steep and narrow for jeeps even. To get to the lighthouse, we climbed and climbed and climbed until the village below was nothing except for a scattering of tiny white dots like breadcrumbs at the edge of the rich blue sea. You could see the Sicilian mainland very clearly on the horizon, and the other Egadi Islands, Marettimo and Favignana too.

Synnøve was working on her new dance recital, she showed me her notebook which was full of Labanotation – her friend Genevieve was going to dance the lead with Enos in support. Her piece is based on Hans Christian Andersen's The Red Shoes – the one about the girl who can't stop dancing when her shoes take control of her; she is bewitched by a soldier who puts a spell on her beautiful red footwear. She dances and dances and nothing she can do can halt the movement of the shoes. At some point, she goes to an executioner to get her feet chopped off with an axe, yet even after he has done his part, the shoes dance on, tormenting her, amputated feet as well. I'm not sure how she is going to adapt it, but I think that's what she has come to Levanzo for, to spend time coming up with a story, and to spend time with me.

On the walk back down from the lighthouse, Enos stumbled on the track and rolled down a steep bank into a small copse of gnarly olive (I think) trees. He called back up to us to say he was OK, but that he'd found something weird. When we all asked what he could see, he just told us to come and see for ourselves. It was one hell of a scramble down the slope but when we went under the tree canopy, we found Enos looking up at this turquoise green copper statue of a man. It was a good seven or eight foot tall, and the effigy had a quill in its right hand and the other hand posed at its lips as if smoking an invisible cigarette. Beatrice was the most amazed, she told us we'd found the stolen statue of Dante Alighieri. It had been missing from the Villa Regina Margherita, a city park in Trapani, for about fifteen years. How it had gotten there was a mystery, as there was seemingly no easy way into the gully. Enos tried to tip it over, but it wouldn't budge. I leant on it, and it was as solid as the tree branches that were hiding it. When we went back to the pensione, Beatrice explained to the owner what we had found, but the woman shook her head and said it was impossible. However, Carlo from the restaurant agreed it could indeed be the stolen statue but in the end, he only had the same questions as us, but he did ask us to show him where it was the next day.

The moon was gigantic that night, it reflected in the sea, double the light; I couldn't see the man in the moon though, he wasn't there. The next morning, Synnøve and I were woken by a host of voices coming up from the sea promenade below our open windows. When we looked out, we could see a crowd of about twenty villagers standing around outside leaning on the sea wall, along the pathways; some of them turned to look as we appeared at the window. Enos and Beatrice were already downstairs waiting for us when we finally left the room after a light breakfast. Carlo, greeted us and said everybody wanted to see the statue with their own eyes. The islanders had packed themselves picnics and carried brightly coloured parasols and they wore big sunglasses – most of them were very old and had very good, leathery tans. There was no use in telling them all it was a steep climb followed by a scramble to get down the slope to where the statue was hidden, it was their island. They knew the journey and they didn't want to listen, they only wanted to talk (and walk). There was one man who tried to explain in a mixture of English and Italian that he could be asleep next week, so the day trip would do him and his friends a lot of good. When Death comes to get me, he will find me wherever I happen to be, so I will go where I want to go, capiche? he said. Nothing can stop me. Beatrice was way ahead in the crowd; it was almost as if she was avoiding being our interpreter. I just felt crap shrugging my shoulders and smiling like I understood everything, but what could I do? There was an old lady who wanted to touch my hair and face a lot, and she just said the name Linda over and over again, which made me feel a bit uncomfortable to tell you the truth. Enos whispered to me that there had to be someone in the crowd who knew how Dante had got there or could even be the ones to have stolen it in the first place – everybody looked so ancient though. I couldn't see anybody remotely fit enough to haul a statue weighing at least a ton to a remote, hilly part of a tiny island. It took over two hours to walk to where it had been hidden. Three quarters of the villagers stayed up on the ridge above the gully, but the remainder managed to make it down into the woods. Carlo confirmed it was, indeed, the stolen statue. He smiled and said a true Sicilian mystery had been solved – he suspected the Mafia may have been behind it, but it wasn't really their style to kidnap statues. Beatrice translated Carlo as saying the puzzle wasn't fully resolved however, because nobody seemed to know how the statue had got there and who had left it in such a strange place. Or indeed, why? He laughed and shrugged, he explained he was just happy it had been found. Yet he was now very concerned the public would think the people of Levanzo were unscrupulous thieves. Everybody filed back to the village, it took ages. It felt like a real outing, a particularly old man called Vincenzo asked me to light his cigarette and then he shared his cheese and tomato sandwiches with me. They were wrapped in a blue and white gingham handkerchief and the bread was so light and fluffy. I had some red wine from a plastic white cup and watched the sun replicated a million times on the distant blue sea far below us.

When we arrived back at the bar in Levanzo Harbour, Carlo and Beatrice phoned the police. Carlo informed us, via Beatrice, and those sitting in the bar, that a detective would come to the island the following week, but we realised we would be back in England by then. Carlo promised to keep in touch with Beatrice so she could let us know what happened next. Sadly, Beatrice became a sleeper on our last night in Levanzo. Luckily, her family lived in Marsala and were able to see her home via the ferry and an ambulance, but we never heard the outcome.

On the penultimate night in Levanzo, which turned out to be the last night the four of us were together, Enos kissed me again. He was a bit drunk and was full of reasons/excuses for his unwelcome behaviour, even though he was far from aggressive or insistent. He thought he could justify his indiscretion by telling me he thought it was OK to kiss somebody you liked as it was a nice thing to do for somebody even if they loved somebody else. I hadn't stopped him at first because it did feel good; our kiss lasted for about a minute before he moved away; it's like I was in a trance and he snapped me out of it when he focused his gaze on me and smiled. He reached his right hand out and placed it lightly on my hip and I took a step backwards. That was the end.

This all brought Lance to the forefront of my mind, and I didn't feel good about treating him this way. I'd had a few glasses of wine and was feeling good about our time in Sicily and it seemed OK, a kiss is small. But the longer I thought about it as the minutes passed, the more wretched I felt. I imagined how upset I would be if I found out Lance was kissing somebody else. It's basic, but I wouldn't feel happy at all as it's a betrayal of trust, nonetheless. Lance and I, we're together. Enos was wrong to kiss me. The enjoyable act alone doesn't make it OK. Later on, in my notebook, I drew a line through Enos's name on the list of men I trust and transferred him into the opposite column.

Hope | Coming any day...

I've been working on a few pencil or charcoal sketches of the sleepers at the racecourse recently, including a drawing of Imogen. None of the nurses or carers seemed to mind, or they're just too busy to even notice. I think my favourite so far is the pencil rendition of Joanne I completed; she is the old lady who was the amanuensis that lived in Dorney. She looked very peaceful as I captured her face on my drawing pad. Joanne has nobody to look after her, but as she lives at the care home nowadays, Mum told me they would be moving her back there. Joanne is one of Mum's favourites.

I like to watch Mum brush the old ladies' locks. She compliments them as she does it, about how smooth their hair is, how it bounces, how elegant it makes them look in the light. Even though some of the 'inmates' have dementia and can't follow what Mum's saying all the time, they can tell she's being kind. Watching her interact with these old people makes me think of when I was a little girl, and the way she would soothe me back to sleep if I woke up from nightmares. How she used to take my face into her shoulder and stroke my hair as she softly shhh'd me back to calmness. Unlike some of the other carers, Mum's sincere. Sincerity is rare in general, I think. She's a really good carer.

I try not to think about it, about my turn to be old – but sometimes I stop and wonder, how will I go? Will it be in an accident, or will I linger like Joanne until I can't even remember my own name, or my mum or dad. Then again, I probably have more to fear from the near future – what might be coming any day. All we ever do is push these immediate things we fear away from us. We think it's happening somewhere else to somebody else, so why should we care? I can still do what I always do. I still have to go to work tomorrow, I have a job, there's nobody stopping me from going outside to see my friends, yet there's this. A fucking hospital taking up the same amount of space as a racecourse that wasn't even here four weeks ago, and now we're all acting like it's normal. Are we adapting, or simply burying our heads in the sand? It's well weird and I'm trying my best not to freak out. This epidemic has spread to every single last corner of the world but we're all so calm and I don't know why? We're docile like cows stoned on the grass they chew. But there's nothing to do except go on or perhaps that's the sleepers' surreptitious message, you don't have to go on. You can just sleep. Join us.

The Chorus | Terrible hubris...

Recently, I got into a conversation with my father about the extinction of dogs and he said something interesting about how short-sighted we all can be. That different species of creatures have been going extinct at a rapid rate since the beginning of time, whether it's through over-hunting, human expansion, a catastrophic change to their environment, or evolution. He stated that human ignorance and avarice combined with terrible hubris has led us all to ignore anything we can't relate to. Our efforts to preserve have often been slow because our governments only work for short term gains and they'll say anything to guarantee their next election. On the other hand, the public at large don't care enough unless the problem is on their doorstep – they have to see the chaos before their own eyes in order to relate and act accordingly; also the chaos has to have a direct and negative impact on their needs. I asked him for an example of an extinction we've all missed. My father took some time out to look at the hills opposite; the three o'clock goods train sounded its horn down in the pass. After some thought he came back to me with one.

The Chorus | You'd notice less

Years and years back, when going down to Cornwall was a huge voyage, I'm talking back before the motorways had fully linked up, you'd arrive at your holiday camp destination and the front of your car – the grille, the headlights, the windscreen, would be coated in dead insects by the hundred. You'd have to spend serious time wiping their obliterated corpses off every surface; it had to be done pretty much right away so they didn't dry out and get hard to shift – their gore damaging your paint job.

As the years went by, you'd notice less and less the need to do this. Nowadays, I never have to do it, after hours of driving there's nary a single bug.

Gene | No dreams...

The papers said some people are waking up. But not as many as the number of those falling asleep every day. There was an interview on the David Frost Show with one of 'the awakened', an Australian lady called Morag or something. She was pretty candid the way she reported that she simply had no lasting memories from her time asleep, she said it was like the time she had been put under for an operation – the whole period was simply missing. There were no dreams, no sensations. Morag went on to admit she was very, very afraid it would happen again, that next time she would fall asleep forever. However, in the roundup at the end of the programme there were other former sleepers who had retained details of their dreams; these talking heads somehow seemed crazier, more wired than Morag, less reliable and eager to bullshit because they were in the spotlight. The most interesting of them was a doctor from Thailand who said he dreamt he was tumbling at incredible speed through a blue sky towards a rocky plain that never got any closer. He spoke of smaller forgotten dreams within the larger dream but the plummet through the vault in flapping robes was always there – hour after hour for three weeks – how he kept on waking up from the inner dreams only to find himself still in endless freefall.

After David Frost had finished, I switched channels and watched an episode of Def II - Behind the Beat followed by Dance Energy; both sometimes showcase good hip hop and the presenter of the latter, Normski, is a bit of a knob but I like laughing at how wack he is, especially his over-the-top reactions to how people are dressed.

Hope | Like witches…

Beetroot and I spent the night in his van. After watching the moon rise and the shadows blackening off the trees around the van, we got off with one another slowly and intensely at first, then we sped up; there must have been something in the atmosphere. We tried to go all the way, the back of the van was so hot, we were slick with sweat; but Beetroot got carried away too early. I thought it was quite funny because he tried to put the head of his cock in my belly button, and he just splatted himself all over my stomach; it was like this massive spunk volcano. We kept on finding new sticky bits all night. It was super gross. He swore me to secrecy, but I joked I'd broadcast it on the CB radio to all the Car Freaks. I think he believed me because he just rolled over and turned his back on me and fell asleep – he snores like a cow and sulks like a hippo.

In the morning, we drove to a lorry drivers' café on the Colnbrook Bypass, and I had a fried egg sandwich and a Pepsi. Beetroot had a full-English and about three coffees. I was glad when I got home because I could finally have a shower and get rid of my dirty clothes and my laddered tights. We both stank like witches.

Gene | Dust in the wind....

Bob and Boodlal invited me to Horsemoor Green Youth Centre which has a small recording studio. They wanted me to make a demo with them and dedicate it to Manjit, who hasn't come around yet. Boodlal's sister Amina is going to sing on it, I think she's a bit rubbish, but I don't want to slate her to the others. I suggested recording her singing something unaccompanied then building the tune around her but they all thought I was dissing her. But I think it makes sense that if someone can't sing you can play the music so that it's in tune with the vocalist, it's like reverse engineering – that's probably what Depeche Mode and New Order do because their singers are tone deaf or flat but their voices suit the songs they make perfectly. We could just use a snippet of her voice a few seconds long and loop it to make something killer... Maybe the song will turn out OK, but they'll just do it the way the want to do it regardless – I have fuck-all influence. I got them to promise to write 'thanks' to me on the label or sleeve, if it gets as far as getting pressed. I think they are aiming for something with a Deee-Lite or S'Express kind of vibe. It's a bit sell-out but it's for a good cause and they want to hit the local dancefloors with it. Oh yeah, it's called, When You Gonna Wake Up? and scratches up The Roof is on Fire by Rockmaster Scott. On the way back from the youth centre, we dropped Boodlal and Amina off in the middle of Slough and then me and Bob went to The Pit. It was mid-afternoon on a Sunday, so White Hart Road was empty. We didn't have our paints with us; we just had a can of Tennent's each – found a flatbed truck to chill inside and then we just talked about a bunch of different samples on records and how he hoped to get his and Boodlal's record on sale at the local record shops and maybe even Our Price. Boodlal is an excellent guitarist – he introduced me to this song called Maggot Brain by Funkadelic. One afternoon, we all got fucked up smoking his gear, just listening to that one song on a loop. I told him that he should teach himself to play it and he said it's probably one of the hardest tunes to play (well) on an electric guitar. Bob began to talk about sleepers and the end of the world, I just listened as his voice got quieter the more I drank. He ended his musings by saying that we're all just dust in the wind, dude. To which I answered, SohCrates!... God bless Bill and Ted.

Bob has a crush on Astrid, but she most probably just sees him as this guy who's out and about on nights out. He always strikes up a conversation with her, to ask her how she's doing, but beyond that, he's like a wet cigarette. Bob's not the type of guy to talk filthy shit about how sexy a girl is with other guys and how he'd like to do this or that to her and I'm not saying that they're the type of guys to score lots of girls; guys like that are low and pretty sad most of the time. But Bob's too far the other way though. He has that romantic, saviour kind of groove. He thinks girls are for wooing and winning, when a lot of the time, that's all the stuff that makes them stay, not what makes them sign up in the first place. He's not all that ugly either, just regular looking I suppose. He's got this big clump of hair, cool Italian glasses, and he keeps his clothes nice but still, some guys just don't appeal to girls in 'that' way. I don't know what it is, they just don't see Bob as boyfriend material, they'd sooner have him around as this dumb kind of eco-friendly fluffy eunuch friend (ha ha)! He's like a dopey donkey on a rope.

All this reminds me of this guy I went to college with called Steve (Timotei) Peddley – the girls all loved him, but the guys really didn't – he was really annoying. And pretty much every single girl on our course slept with him (I know of eight for sure who went down the road with him during the two years I was there). It's like one of them did it with him and then went and told all the others, hey, you must really give this guy a go… or something – it's like when you see everybody reading the same book just because it's a best-seller – Steve was a fad and we all really, really wished it was us. Thinking about it sensibly for a second, I guess it saved the girls from having crap sex with their close male friends, all the ones that reminded them of their brothers (ha ha); the ones they couldn't bear to lose by getting intimate with them. Giving up the boody to Timotei seemed like a large-scale solution to this problem – I mean, I think girls are pretty unimaginative in the main, and this was a really good example of weak minds failing to differ on a massive scale – I mean they all pretty much lined up to jump on his willy like it was whack-a-mole – they most probably even compared notes. All these hordes of horny female art students experienced a sudden fear of missing out. They just had to try Timotei out for themselves if only to fit in. It was pretty baffling to witness when so many of us other lads had capacity – even my mates who already had girlfriends were disgusted at our female friends' lack of ingenuity or originality. I've never met anyone else like Steve who had that kind of, I don't know what you'd call it, luck or pull but he had it. He wasn't all that good looking either; he had this silky-looking long brown hair, a chubby face like Andrew Lloyd-Webber, and he went around town on a tiny, shit Yamaha 250LC. He'd always wear moccasin shoes and this jacket with suede off-the-arm tassels and a great big spread-wing American eagle on the back – he should have been in TV's Highway to Heaven. One time, he came to class dressed in his taekwondo dobok, slippers and all (which just set the girls off even more) he was one thousand percent naff, man. Softly-spoken, he was a real bore to us guys – we'd make snoring noises whenever he asked one of his really long questions in class. He got his nickname, Timotei, because of the way he'd shake his mane of clean hair out of his crash helmet. We think he probably wore mail order animal pheromones; it was the only logical explanation for his success. After college wrapped up, he moved back to the Isle of Sheppey to live with his nan; he probably needed to give his dick a bit of a lie down. Anyway, in short, Bob is living proof girls don't give a stuff about nice guys like him. They really don't care whether you are kind and a good listener, they don't give a shit about any of that good shit, they are just interested in keeping up with what all the other girls are doing so they don't stand out or get left behind, and this is what makes so many of them a bit boring to me – this pack mentality, zzz.

When me and Bob were leaving The Pit, we caught a whiff of fresh paint and then saw this still-wet mural of a galloping dog of some kind on the side of a yellow double-decker with flat tyres. The words, And the years run like rabbits – WH Auden, had been written underneath in a cursive script made with a stencil – it seemed to dance in the torch's beam. We didn't say much, we just looked and smiled at the artistry. It was blatantly Slave. We'd missed him by minutes.

Rowan | Not going along…

Since Warren got me transferred off the beds department, I've been working on toys and games. It's mainly man-boys with stupid animal faces and angry dumpy women with dead short hair and beer bellies who work up there. There's this really fussy guy called Allen who speaks from the back of his throat like he's being strangled. He wears a mauve suit daily along with a matching tie complementing his electric white shirts – he's even got a lint roller – I've seen him use it several times. Also, I think he trims his moustache and eyebrows daily, and maybe even the fringe of his massive apple-shaped bowl of brown hair. He does everything at one speed, smoothly and precisely like he's an automaton. Sometimes, I have to cover him for lunch, and when he comes back after he's eaten, he dusts everything and puts all of his things like the card swiper and his pens back to exactly the same way he'd left them an hour earlier. He knows his stuff about Hornby Trains, Scalextric, and Airfix model kits, he's a mastermind, but I don't see the appeal – men and their collections and obsessions, this need they have to label and list things that have no point or substance.

One morning, Allen's wife and two sons came in to say hello to him, and they weren't what I expected to see at all. They were all dressed in bright clothes and were bubbly and smiling. She was a fair bit younger than him and was really nice to me when I was introduced to her. Her name was Jan, Sam, or Ann – it was noisy when she told me. She wore her hair in dreadlocks, and she complimented my braids. She was wearing blue eye shadow and had a piercing in her left eyebrow and henna patterns on her long hands. Maybe Allen saves his ordered way of life for work, and lets chaos rule at home, as I can't imagine him having a neat house because she looks like a free spirit and not one to take any shit; I mean that in a nice way. Allen never talks about her to me, and I didn't notice him smile at her when they spoke together – they are the oddest couple I've ever seen in my life.

The dimbos from the loading bay were in the canteen, they had The People open on an article saying some men had been arrested for raping a girl in her sleep. The sick fucks were even joking about it. I complained to their supervisor that I thought it was really out of order. I mean, what if it had been their girlfriend, sister or mum? Nobody is putting themselves into anybody else's shoes. They are just going along as normal until it's their turn. Apes! One of them actually apologised to me, but I said it's not a matter of saying sorry, it's a matter of not going along with your mates if they are being dicks, he just said he was sitting at the table minding his own business eating his Ringos and he'd felt like I was making him into an accomplice simply by being there.

Later on, this kid called Nils, the one who was reading the article out loud, called me a bitch and barged past me in the hallway by the locker room, but Allen saw it happen and got a grip of him by the hood of his parka and swung him around, and asked if I was OK, and he demanded Nils say sorry to me, which he did. I still find Allen irritating, but he went up a few notches in my eyes after that.

The Chorus | A borrowed protection...

The dogs didn't want to leave us, I'm certain of it. If they still could, they would be pining for us the same way we are for them. They had no choice in the matter, they had no time to say goodbye to us either. Think how animals protect themselves purely out of instinct, if a predator is on their trail, how it will escape being captured, how a trapped wild animal like a hare or a fox may even chew through its own leg to free themselves from a snare; our dogs wanted to remain by our sides, they didn't want to go, they tried to hang on as long as they could. Their loyal presence lulled us into believing things stay the same forever, that days like the ones we had together would never end, but it all mutates, everything, it all moves slowly on. We need to ask ourselves why we only seem capable of seeing this whole horrible situation from a human point of view?

Hope | Beginning to wake

I have a shift at Eton Wick Services today. Casey is acting manager now because Ash is a sleeper as of last week. In some ways, Casey is stricter, but she respects us more and seems fairer, and I know she doesn't set traps in the tills, so in a few days I'll begin to take a few quid here and there – steal big, steal little but then I'm bound to get found out if I don't stop as there's only me, Casey, Gene and Beetroot in now. I asked Casey when she was going to go to Australia, and she said she wanted to make sure Ash was OK before she went off. She didn't want him to wake up only to find out she had vanished off to the Land Down Under. The last time they had been together she said it had been lovely, they'd gone to Pizza Hut in Cippenham for a meal. Afterwards they went for a nice floaty kind of walk thing in Burnham Beeches. They'd talked about the future, and, for the first time, they'd held hands in public – she admitted she was really keen on him, and I was happy for her even though Ash is a total penis. Casey asked Gene to man the tills and then we had a heart-to-heart in the stockroom. She cried quietly and told me she hadn't even said goodbye properly, she didn't even stand outside her flat to watch him drive off because she was feeling a bit cold. She wished she'd invited him inside so they could have spent more time together. I tried to comfort her. Casey then explained it wasn't the not knowing and the waiting that would kill her, but whether or not her bad goodbye was her final goodbye. I really believe everybody will return to normal again. I reminded her that people everywhere were beginning to wake up again, not many but a few, and the numbers of those awakened would improve. I assured her she'd see Ash again; I don't think we are on a path of no return, but it's difficult to believe that at times. I wonder if I'm in denial.

The Chorus | Our vainglorious stories…

The dogs evolved to domesticate us and not the other way around – our vainglorious stories tell us we tamed them to stop them from being ferocious killers of men, that we halted their ascent to apex predator by giving them fireside scraps and getting them to hunt for us and with us. However popular this way of looking at our doggy dominance is, I don't subscribe to it. I think it's the dogs who drew us to them in the first instance, they offered us their warm companionship, a borrowed protection, they are the ones who helped us find flora and fauna to eat in the winter by offering their knowledge and skills up for mutual benefit.

Did you know dogs evolved to have eyebrows so they could appeal to us when it's time to eat – they changed to enhance their expressions and anthropomorphise themselves in order to develop our synergetic relationship beyond a working one? The dogs had even schooled themselves and us to raise our oxytocin levels. But in the process of finding warmth and food together, we found love and respect too and this is what still hurts so much about the dogs' leaving. It's this aching obsession I have with what is absent. The lack of their presence is akin to living hundreds of miles inland and still being aware of the ceaseless sea rolling in at the coast under the cover of night and in the glare of day – its turning and turning over like a drugged demon in dreams.

Gene | At any time...

I was reading in the papers earlier that some shops, restaurants and sections of the travel networks are struggling to stay open because of the lack of staff around to replace the sleepers. People are either inexperienced, already in work, or they don't see the point in training up or taking a job when they themselves could fall asleep at any time, so posts remain open. Bob said he didn't see why they had to be so defeatist. So many people seem resigned to accept they are going to become a sleeper. But I see their point, bollocks to it, everything is pointless to me.

Casey said it was quite likely our hours would get reduced as most of the food stands inside Eton Wick Service don't open up anymore. The only ones still going are Wimpy on our side and McDonalds on the eastbound side; Parminder's only got one person left working with her on the other side, but their shop is half the size of ours. Customers still drop in for their newspapers and a can of pop and that's it but soon even the papers may end up slowing down.

The big front-page news today is that Brian Keenan has been

released in Lebanon but he's asleep. He got handed over last night – I can imagine his captors just rolling his bed down a hill over the border into Syria before running off into the alleys – Keenan still fast asleep under the blankets.

I'm thinking of leaving work because I don't want to see the end of the world arrive from behind a cash register – either way, if we're going to last or we're going to go all the way out, I want to have experienced something of it for myself. I want to see what's happening in the cities. The rallies in London are getting more and more violent and they occur daily now. The army and the police have been in clashes with students and ordinary people outside the Houses of Parliament, Trafalgar Square, 10 Downing Street and all over. They, scrap that, *we!,* we just want answers. The people want to know what's next, but the MPs (cowardly criminals that they are) just hide out in their bunkers flicking bogeys at each other. Nothing's happening but I don't think I'm scared. Beetroot told me the Car Freaks listen to army manoeuvres on their CB radios. And we talked about becoming roving reporters for the M Brothers Show to let our listeners know when the boot was coming down. We said we could be anonymous and have aliases like The Militant Brothers Sortie or something appropriate. At the moment, the Car Freaks listen to comms on an unpopular bandwidth but can pick up radio chatter of troop movements out of Victoria and Combermere Barracks in Windsor and also TA bases as far away as Hounslow. Beetroot said it was quite difficult to interpret without a cipher and that most of the Car Freaks were bored out of their ball sacks and bras already and preferred to listen to music.

The Chorus | Lord of the dance...

Do you remember that old folk hymn we sang in school assembly back in the seventies called Lord of the Dance? It was a big hit for The Dubliners. Does it feel a bit 'behind the door' to compare the sleepers to a religious flock, all of them playing follow the leader like they do in that song; do you think everyone is being spirited away to some alternative mysterious life by some otherworldly conductor? No doubt it's flippant to state this, maybe even unkind, and anybody reading the broadsheets knows it's a medical condition, but I almost feel as if there are swathes of the population willing the sleeping disease upon themselves; it's as if they are welcoming the experience.

I danced on the Sabbath when the sky went black, it's hard to dance with the devil on your back. That line utterly disturbed me as a child, I never realised it was referring to Jesus' crucifix. Bible stories terrified me in primary school, where the teachers sold the tales as fact, and we were taught to believe in supernatural miracles. At the back of my mind, I wish I knew no different – I'd probably be a long-time believer if it was all just song and dance.

Hope | There are more questions than answers...

Carmine's is still closed but the barbershop has been back open for at least a fortnight now. Andrea seems to be his old self, but he can't be, anybody could tell you that. He said the restaurant is going to go up for sale. He wants to sell the barbers too, but he is working to pay back a family loan so he will probably stay behind. He confessed all his friends were around here, and that for as long as he was awake, he'd stay around to cut hair, and all the usual. He told me the situation was quite bad in Italy, that one in fifty people have fallen asleep now, and that everything is on the brink of collapse. He said that in England, we would see an impact more visibly because we don't have siestas, but things are nowhere near as crazy here (yet). Unemployment is down in the UK according to the papers I saw on the seats outside Andrea's Salon, but if you are a sleeper, do you still have your job?, I asked him. He just shrugged and said numbers can be crunched any way to reflect a positive outcome. When it comes down to it, we're all like Johnny Nash he said, then he started to sing There Are More Questions Than Answers which is this old reggae song my dad likes.

Beetroot told me Lance had fallen asleep and was in a temporary hospital on the school field at Langley Grammar. Astrid has only been home from Sicily for a day or so and hadn't even had time to see him. She's beside herself. I will walk over to her house later to see if she wants company or needs somebody to talk to.

Astrid | If we could go…

Lance, my Bajan boy, I never thought you would become a sleeper. Nobody knows when you will wake up. I'm bereft.

Lance is at the new temporary hospital at Langley Grammar as he has nobody to look after him all the time as he lives alone. His mum is a cow and has nothing to do with him really and his dad lives in Barbados. Perhaps now, they will care about what happens to him.

I was only home from Sicily one day and I spoke to Lance on the phone as soon as I got home from the airport but kept it short because I was really tired. He asked me if I wanted to go to his, or if we could go for a drive. But it was no good, I couldn't even function after all the waiting around in airport lounges and bus shelters, so I told him that although I wanted to see him very much, all I had wanted to do was lie in my own bed and sleep. Mum and Crap Craig kept me up talking for a while, asking questions about the holiday. Synnøve told them about the statue beneath the trees, but I excused myself and went to bed. I don't even know how Synnøve can hold a conversation with that arsehole Craig. He woke me up about an hour later when he fired up the engine on his over-compensating flash car and drove off home.

I keep on asking myself, what if I had gone out with Lance the other night, would he be okay? I've been crying for two days straight now. I should be going through my reading list, but I can't focus. I just want to be with him. Synnøve has been really good about it and has gone to Langley with me on the bus a few times, and she's never even met Lance properly.

Hope | A forgotten tale…

I came across a sketch I did of Luca last year during the summer holidays. He was sitting outside Andrea's barbershop having a haircut right there on the street: a clump of his hair blew in through the bakery next door and pissed the owner, Helen, off, she came out yelling, turning the air blue! It wasn't an ideal setup for me either because they kept on moving about and laughing. Luca and Andrea were both trying to tell me a story about something that had happened to them, but they kept on interrupting each other. Andrea was laughing at something Luca had done, but Luca was correcting him, saying Andrea was making everything up. The whole tale revolved around Andrea and Luca's attempt to ask this waitress out for a drink with them. In the end they succeeded in persuading her but she was pissed off because she thought she was saying yes to a date with Luca and not Andrea. And when the latter showed up instead, she just turned around and went back home. The famous case of the wrong brother.

I Blu-Tacked the sketch of Luca on my bedroom wall. Then I squiggled my signature in the bottom left-hand corner followed by the words Summer '89 (T-minus one year). It's been so warm the Blu-Tack has dried out and the picture has kept falling off the wall and onto my bed.

Gene | A limitation exercise…

I've pretty much walked out of my job; they're a load of clowns. I work a week-in-hand, so I probably won't get paid, but the money is squid piss anyway. I took a box of crisps and copies of Hip Hop Connection, Echoes, and Blues & Soul to make up for it.

I've decided I'm going up to London on the train to take part in the protests on Saturday. I don't know what's going to happen, nobody does. The train is the only effective way to get into London they reckon, the M25 is being used as a wall to keep the worst of the trouble inside. I wonder what it's like for commuters, if people are still going into their offices every day. It's not like you can work from home – I wouldn't fucking risk it but then all those twats in the bowler hats probably deserve a Molotov cocktail chucked at them, or to get their smug grey faces kicked in. Have the army use them for target practice – re-route their packed trains and have them all plummet off the White Cliffs of Dover – mashed into a beige paste on the rocks below. Anyway, the capital has been partially cut off by the forces as a containment/limitation exercise but London's massive and the army's not that big – what can they do to stop those who have remained standing, walking, not sleeping? They won't be able to keep us all out or in, there's got to be loads of ways in and out on foot, then you could steal a car or a bike once you are in Acton or somewhere.

I want to see an anarchists' flag flying from the top of Big Ben; I want to see Maggie Thatcher's head on the end of a sharp stick, establish a new Tyburn for wealthy crooks and right-wing Tories; I want to see it all burn to a crisp in a slow fury.

I miss my Mum.

The Chorus | Those strange rooms...

One of my saddest regrets is not staying with Heidi right up to the end. She was very old and in immense pain from an inoperable tumour. The sense of an ending was too apparent to ignore so we took her to the vet for the final time. It was too much to bear so we left her in the surgery and the vet's assistant took her away. I heard the door to the room close and then she was gone. I didn't stop to think about it until an hour or two later, how frightened she would have been without us in that strange room. I'd put myself first by valuing my own self-preservation over my Heidi's anxious state. And I didn't even stop and think about how confused and scared my beautiful love would have been in her last moments; she wanted me to be there, to stroke her fur, to be beside her as she slipped under. She didn't want to go, she wanted to be with me forever. And I didn't want her to go.

Astrid | The tilt of their ovals...

I first met Lance last summer, he was hanging around with some boys at the end of Haywards Mead. They were all sitting in and on this big white car with spoilers and mods and they were listening to some house tune I knew but couldn't name. Anyway, I tried not to get spotted looking at him, but he caught my eye. He's not conventionally handsome but there was something there. You know like when you hear a certain kind of melody in a song or detect an unexpected yet welcome flavour in a drink you like, well, there's a particular face I seek out to give me that same inkling. It's just an essence of something, I can't articulate it properly, but Lance had it. The spacing of their eyes, the tilt of their ovals, the cheekbones or lack of, a feeling of familiarity in the unfamiliar. I felt as though I'd seen him before even though I hadn't. Perhaps I'd thought this boy up and then there he was; he looked like the idea I'd had of 'a' boyfriend in my head even before I'd seen him, so that day when I saw him, I felt like I had to know who he was. Old eyes on a new country.

I asked Imogen and Rowan if they knew him, and they didn't.

They teased me, as I had never expressed any kind of interest in boys (to their knowledge) before. Imogen said she'd find out and as we walked down to the river to dip our feet in the flow, she went and talked to them. When she caught up with us a bit later, she told me she'd written my telephone number down for this guy, his name was Lance and he said he'd call. Imogen described him as a 'nice' boy which translated as tame and not her type. A day or so later, I came home from shopping and there was a scribbled note saying Lance had phoned and left his number, meaning it was now down to me to move it all forwards. I know this all sounds quite ordinary, so I won't string it out for much longer, but when we did eventually get our act together, we met for a drink at the Two Brewers by the gates to The Long Walk in Windsor. Afterwards, we went for a stroll to the Copper Horse which was just over two miles each way. As a kid I always thought it felt like me, Mum, and Synnøve were going on a trek into the desert or something – we'd pack our bags full of lunch, eight million cans of pop, carrier bags of fruit and crisps and we'd make a real day of it. Lance and I had nothing with us but our stories, and we just hit it off really well. He was quiet, respectful and when my mum met him a few weeks later she told him he had a kind face. He does. She saw what I saw on that first day. She saw the same thing.

If I could, I would promise him, really promise him that everything is going to be OK. That it's all going to come out fine. I want it to be.

The Chorus | Combined into a force...

I keep on hearing the words 'loot the lot' as well as seeing it written on walls around the city. What does looting achieve? The shops are still open, fruit is still growing on the trees, people are are still choosing to start families – then why rob and pillage? I don't understand that spark of agency, the urge to smash and destroy innocent people's property just to make a political statement.

Mob rule is an impressive thing to behold, you rarely see humans act as anything other than individual organisms, so seeing them move en masse to benefit the same cause is rare; a riot is a mash of minds and bodies combined into a single force. Each individual is empowered by a sense of belonging to something much bigger and stronger than themself, that they're in the crux of a powerful entity. You can strike out and be absorbed back into the anonymous safety of the group – throw a brick through a window, a Molotov cocktail at a mounted policeman – it wasn't you, it was the crowd – your actions backed by the throng. In the end though, the messages get lost or garbled, and the fighters are ultimately condemned for barbarism by the government you're all railing against – they point score and say they welcome discussion not destruction – government agents are sent to infiltrate the protest movement because they hate us as much as we hate them – the crusade subverted and hijacked by random acts of mayhem. The cycle begins again. The articulate complain, the brutes set out to crush. We're falling asleep and we want to steal from those we should be protecting. Whether or not we will be of interest to future generations will never be a concern to us, we need to work on discarding our feudal spirit or it's a zero-sum game.

Astrid | A warm sea...

What if the best version of yourself exists in somebody else's head? If I don't get to speak with you ever again, how will you ever know I carry an unbeatable version of you within me?

I can hardly keep you out Lance and I don't want to remember you wrongly. There's a possibility you will never know the 'you' I live in like a warm sea.

I wrote the above on a small piece of paper in block capitals. Then I folded it up and put it into Lance's left palm, then I closed his hand. I felt his breath on my knuckles as I withdrew my hand from his cheek. When I went in to see him a few hours later the note was no longer in his hand, I looked on the floor and in the bed around him, but it was wasn't there.

Synnøve told me not to mistake my vigil for mourning because Lance was simply sleeping, that he's going to come back to me. I know this but it doesn't feel like a truth, it feels like an urgent wish.

The papers today are reporting that the WHO were now referring to the sleep condition as a conversion disorder. The journalists explained it was similar to a fainting fit and mass hysteria, where the public is simply reacting to what everybody else is doing and that our brains are processing it as an illness, when really, everything is in our minds like a perverse magic trick. I've jotted bits down to help me get it all clear in my head and so I can talk about it in plain English and not end up getting myself in knots. Even though the sleep sickness is being classed as a medical condition the confusion has arisen because the medical language used to describe it has yet to exist; it's currently difficult to outline its ins-and-outs. According to doctors and experts they are being set back by bad dynamics and outdated language that is unsuitable for explicitly sharing precisely what's happening. As I understand it, although the cause may be different from person to person, the outcome is the same in everybody. A sleeper is habitually reacting to their origin issue on a subconscious level based on old experiences the same way animals do. It's something each and every single one of us has coded into our psyches simply by living and there is nothing we are able to do except resist it whether we fall asleep or not. Many people are taking these explanations literally and have begun to find ways to stay really awake. Some take artificial stimulants; others are setting their alarm clocks at fifteen-minute-gaps throughout the night. Those trying to go without sleep, fall asleep after two days only to wake up extremely tired the next morning as normal – although some of these people have become sleepers.

Obviously, I've been spending a lot of time at the hospital, so there's been lots of time and opportunity to read discarded newspapers and magazines. I said I'd been avoiding the news, but it doesn't look like turning my back on the whole situation is an option any longer. I feel as though I've been the one sleepwalking.

Rowan | Exotic trees…

Mum is worried in case the danger in London spills out this way towards Eton Wick, she reckons it will because it has spread the same way in other countries. The M25 is being closed off by the army so no traffic gets in or out – there's just reduced public transport; as if that's going to work – how can all the roads be closed? There are hundreds of them. Riots have broken out everywhere, almost daily – places like Bristol, Birmingham, Manchester, Liverpool, Newcastle, and yesterday Plymouth and Bournemouth.

A group of louts set trees on fire at this famous arboretum in The Cotswolds last night, all these lovely rare trees burnt to a cinder. I saw this hell on the TV at breakfast. They are just letting it burn until nothing's left – the fire service has been told to get on with supporting the army against rioting in built-up areas – they don't give a shit because they just assume the trees will grow back or they just don't care.

Gene | Crushed from all sides...

I went into London with Bob, Beetroot, and Hope to see what was happening – I didn't tell the others, but I was bricking it. I had to make myself sick in the toilets at Slough Railway Station just to calm my nerves. We all shared a can of Tennents on the platform before we got on the train – when Beetroot called it Dutch courage it reminded me of GCSE History when they told us about soldiers in the First World War each getting a shot of rum before they went 'over the top'. I felt like I was flushed with a fever or something; my temperature was yo-yo-ing and I felt woozy.

The trains only go as far as Ealing Broadway or Richmond this side of London, so we had to get buses into the heart of the capital. Bob was the only one of us who was really up for it and that was just so he could go record shopping. He told me both Groove and Hitman Records were having clearout sales before temporarily closing down until the madness had ground to a halt. I fancied buying some tunes as well, but I only had enough scratch for food and fares. I suppose if I found a bank open, I could take out more.

We could smell Westminster before we saw it. Where there

used to be a big green opposite the Westminster Hall and the Houses of Parliament there was now a colossal bonfire, hundreds of tents, chaos, people, flames and black smoke everywhere. The crowd was massive and the sound of voices deafening, some were singing Boris Gardiner's I Want To Wake Up With You at the top of their voices; I used to hate that song but since it became the sleeper's anthem, I think it's alright.

We arrived in time for noon, and when the clock chimed the crowd went fucking mental chanting fuck all Tories, loot the lot, and we're not dogs – don't let us die. Everybody on the green was facing towards the River Thames and Big Ben. Everywhere, people were closing in on one another and we were getting crushed from all sides. I'd never seen Beetroot so scared. I began to sing/shout the words to the Boris Gardiner song at the end of my lungs until I began to cough from the smoke. Bottles were thrown at the soldiers and police lined up in front of Westminster Abbey and Parliament. Some people at the front tried to run into the road but the authorities threw tear gas at them – I didn't even know what it was at first until Bob said. We were quite far back but our eyes were streaming, and we were all wheezing and coughing. It was hard to breathe but we just put our heads down and ploughed through the hornets' nest of angry demonstrators until we reached the far edge of the green. Hope fell the minute we reached the pavement, grazing one of her knees on the curb. Beetroot was no longer red, he was blue/purple, his eyes bulging out like peeled eggs. The crowd seemed to calm down again, we could hear coughing, and vomiting all around. I helped Hope to her feet and she smiled although I could tell she was frightened – we all were except for Bob. He was the first to recover properly, he was busy taking photos from the top of a green telecoms box, he gave me a wink, and yelled we're just dust in the wind, dude! That was Bob for you, he didn't nurse things; the rest of us took about an hour to recover. We sat around on various doorsteps not saying anything, and we all shared a big bottle of water Hope had brought with her. Thank God she did. It really helped.

Later on, we made our way past the lines of police and soldiers and bundled ourselves to Trafalgar Square along Whitehall past another knot of angry demonstrators that had gathered around the new Downing Street gates. Again, we had to stop and rest; we just sat in a doorway trying not to vomit anymore and to get our shit together again. Beetroot was the last of us to recover, he just hid under Hope's coat. It was really hard, but Bob kept our spirits up by telling us how we were a part of a movement, part of history, that the photos he was taking would be in the papers.

In Trafalgar Square, the people down there were way more peaceful – we arrived at about three o'clock. I couldn't believe we'd actually arrived by bus at Victoria Station at midday. Time was an onslaught.

All around Nelson's Column and the lion statues, we saw crowds of people holding up photographs of sleeping relatives, others held up pictures of dogs. Again, Boris Gardiner, was playing out of giant speakers the size of one of the stone plinths at each corner of the square; his song will probably be at number one in the charts until all this is over. Here and there, the crowd sang along and whoever controlled the volume knob turned the record down so only our voices could be heard a cappella. I wonder what songs have been championed like this in other countries around the world. In Germany, the people have picked Boris too.

After a while Bob and Beetroot decided to go record shopping in Soho; Hope and I tried to talk them out of it, but Bob's addicted to buying wax, and I think Beetroot just wanted to get away from the crowds, I don't know, he wasn't saying all that much.

At the time we just carried on with the hordes of protestors and listened to speakers talk about the lack of help the government was giving to the poor or anybody really, about the bad side-effects of speed, and tips on trying to stay awake in general. We had arranged to meet Bob and Beetroot on the front steps of the National Gallery two hours after they left but they never showed up. At about seven o'clock, we went to Berwick Street (where all the record shops are) to look for them, but everywhere was either closed for the day or the boys simply weren't there. Quite a few of the shops and pubs were boarded up – LTL spray painted on the hoardings and walls. More words were painted on the tarmac and pavements.

WAKE UP.
EAT THE ROYALS.
WE ARE NOT DOGS.
KILLING US SOFTLY.
I WANT TO WAKE UP WITH YOU (NOT YOU).
FUCK THATCHER SLOWLY.
DON'T CLOSE YOUR EYES.
WHAT'S WRONG WITH THE MOON?
SAY HELLO, WAVE GOODBYE.
THE TRUTH IS OUT
WHY DOES BUGS BUNNY HAVE BIG EARS? COS HE'S

YOUR BROTHER.
DING DONG BELL MAGGIE THATCHER GO TO HELL.
THERE ARE MORE QUESTIONS THAN ANSWERS.
THIS IS A TORY PLANNED PLAGUE!!!
BOY GEORGE ATE MY PUSSY CAT.
JOEY DEACON WAS HERE.
NEIL KINNOCK IS A LESBIAN.
THATCHER, TOM KING, DAVID WADDINGTON, KEN CLARKE, JOHN MAJOR, DO YOUR JOBS YOU FUCKERS – DOGS OVER TORIES.
SAM FOX FOR PRIME MINISTER.
DON'T BEAM ME UP YET SCOTTY, I'M TAKING A SH….

Rowan | Return to her…

I called around for Astrid after work, but Synnøve told me she wasn't home, she spent most her time at the temporary hospital in Langley with Lance. She invited me in, and we sat and shared a cold can of XXXX on the patio and made small talk about a play she was writing about the fairy tale, The Red Shoes. She showed me a few moves and her red ballet shoes, saying that it would all kind of revolve around David Bowie's Let's Dance song, but she thought I was boring her when I was actually fascinated. Unfortunately, I couldn't persuade her that I was into what she had to show me. After her brief display she went quiet for a moment and flashed a demure smile. Synnøve's university course is on hold, and she said she didn't want to return to her flat in London until the riots had calmed down. If I'm going to fall asleep, I want to be here. I'm staying so I can help if Mum or Astrid succumb to the deep sleep disease, she said. Plus, I'm worried for Astrid, she's so different because of Lance.

Synnøve is a bit smaller than Astrid, who is curvier, I guess it's all the dancing – her limbs are very taut, she looks like there's not an ounce of fat on her. She has the clearest blue eyes I've ever seen and the blackest hair. She offered me a cigarette and I took one in lieu of chatter and we watched the early evening sky. After a while, she pointed at the moon and asked whether I thought it looked strange. It just looked bigger as the sky was full of summer dust, a disc of orange and yellow pastel colours. I've never really sat and stared at it before – maybe I'll paint it one day.

I began to wonder what it would be like to walk on the moon – nothing ever changes on the moon. Supposedly, Neil Armstrong's footprints are still there at Tranquility Base uneroded by wind, or rain.

Hope | All you can do…

We couldn't get a train back out of London because they'd all been cancelled until the morning. We thought we'd see Beetroot and Bob at the station, but they weren't there. There were so many people at Ealing Broadway Station; we had to step over all the people lying down, so many people are sleeping rough.

I was completely out of ideas about what to do. Neither Bob nor Beetroot have beepers so basically all we could do was wait. Beetroot always arrives on time for work and is always where we arrange to meet promptly when we're hanging out, so I'm inclined to worry. Gene says Bob is pretty reliable as well, but he doesn't seem as worried. He keeps on checking his watch but has more or less given up on chatting as there's not much left to say. He keeps on repeating that they'll be OK, and I'll reply back, but how do you know? We've gone in circles. They're in control, Bob and Beetroot, all we can do is go home. I wish we hadn't even come up. All I can taste is smoke at the back of my throat, no amount of water or chewing gum is getting rid of the flavour. I got really cold but felt awkward leaning into Gene, as we sat on the platform with our backs against the side wall of the waiting room. We could see all the way down the tracks back towards West London. There was no movement out there, it was like looking at a photograph. I could just see rails and static red lights in the brown dark.

Rowan | Everything outside...

I was woken up in the middle of the night by a huge explosion. Probably gone midnight. It made the knife and fork rattle on the plate next to my bed and my house keys fall off the art desk. It woke Mum too; through the thin wall, I heard her get out of bed and go to the window. I shouted to ask her if she was OK, but she never replied. I waited until I heard her move back and climb back into bed before I went to the window myself. I assumed it was a car crash on the motorway or a factory explosion on Slough Industrial Estate. Everything outside was as it should be, the rows of gardens, the houses opposite; lights had come on in many of the windows.

Next morning the news said a car bomb had gone off outside Windsor Castle, nobody was seriously injured, just lots of broken windows and a half-demolished pub and a tourist gift shop. There were interviews with the few people who saw it blow up, and lots of coverage of the burnt-out van wreckage and Queen Victoria's statue with no head on anymore.

Astrid | Life peels away…

Mum and I went for a walk down the river in Windsor – she persuaded me I needed some time away from watching over Lance.

Nothing hurts this much. Life moves slowly on and everything seems to peel away. Mum has been trying to get me to eat but I can't keep anything down, I just can't swallow anything without retching. I can't.

The area up around the castle has been cordoned off because of a car bomb that went off in the early hours of the morning. Nobody knows who left the device there but there have been several ideas floated in the news although everyone says it's the IRA, but they haven't taken responsibility for it; they usually claim it or say there's a bomb even when there isn't. Another van full of explosives was found in Regent's Park next to London Zoo! Who would want to blow up animals?

My university course has been postponed so my entrance has been indefinitely deferred which is understandable – I probably wouldn't have gone with Lance as he is anyway. I phoned Ash to ask if I could have my job back part-time but Casey's in charge now – nobody had told me that he was a sleeper. Casey told me Gene and Beetroot had walked out, so there was just her and Hope now and I could come back whenever I wanted. This is OK news as I need some routine to keep me strong for Lance, I recognise it's too much to sit at his bedside constantly; I want to though.

Mum has finally told Crap Craig to fuck off out of it. He smashed a few things in the house and gripped my mum around the throat before I smacked him in the back of the head with a videotape. He dropped my mum, stunned and just marched out the house without a word, rubbing his head. That was the night the bomb went off and we haven't seen him since. Hopefully, that's the end of that shit show.

Someone had spray painted the words, the victory of reason is the victory of the reasonable on the outer walls of School Yard at Eton College. Somebody else had daubed de omnibus dubitandum est on the walls lining the road through Eton Fields where they play the wall game. I don't know what it means but I've scribbled these quotes down in my ideas book.

I noticed the army are camped out on Eton Playing Fields now – tents, armoured cars and some tanks parked along the roadsides and on the college's cricket pitches down Pococks Lane. The soldiers stood around at the Burning Bush, with semi-automatic rifles on their hips, left us alone to drive past the Upper School on our way back from our walk. I think the local rag said there are going to be checkpoints going in and out of Eton to protect 'the boys' after they've returned to school next week. Colleges and universities close but Eton plods on. The aristocracy never sleeps – this is the proof.

Hope | Protect the weak…

By the time I got back to Eton Wick, Beetroot still hadn't turned up. I called his house three times and his mum said she hadn't seen him at all, she'd assumed he was working. Like Gene, Beetroot seems to have ditched his job; I can't do that because I need the dosh and I can't leave Casey in the lurch. I am going insane worrying about him though as he was really frightened when we were in Westminster.

When I got on the train from Ealing Broadway, Gene said he wasn't coming back with me, that he was going to carry on looking for Bob and Beetroot. I liked that he stayed with me in the station all night, I slept with my head in his lap, and he kept watch. At sunrise, we talked here and there about what was going to happen, and he said he thought people would most probably do their best to carry on except most people are shit in general, and there's some who will take advantage of the situation by stealing and causing violence. He paused then added more thoughtfully that a minority of others may well come together to protect the weak and all that's good in the world, but he knew ultimately that it would all come down to natural selection, survival of the fittest, smartest and hardest working. I've never really talked to Gene about anything serious, I guess we never see what's obvious about our friends until we're in trouble and that we're never truly tested or pushed to see if we're a good person or the opposite – not really. We never ask that of ourselves, not until the beast is so close to us, He can be seen walking behind our eyelids.

As the train was about to go, Gene gave me a hug and kissed me on the cheek. I tried to hold onto him, but he wrestled himself away and jumped back down to the platform. I wasn't used to seeing him like this, but I guess he was caught up in the sweep of it all, I tried to hold onto him, but he was gone in the knot and pull of people. I want everything to be alright, but I don't know and now, he may as well be missing in London too.

Rowan | Without everybody singing…

Simon P came into Daniels and invited me to a free party at a secret venue in Slough. He said that him and his mates had built some crazy floodlights, and some guys he knew from Bracknell were bringing a sound rig. He was talking all fast and his lips were blue from inhaling some poison, and he was slouching on the till top when Allen came back from his lunch. After Simon left, he sprayed air freshener around and told me that men like 'my friend' were a waste of skin.

The tape at work has a rotation of pop records on it and now I can't get that sodding Boris Gardiner song out of my head, I Want To Wake Up With You. It was shit in the first place without everybody singing it all the time – even the busker in Peascod Street was doing it, out opposite the headless Queen Victoria statue. I don't want to wake up with anybody.

The Chorus | Perfectly healthy...

Did you know ninety eight percent of veterinarians in the UK have been asked to euthanise a perfectly healthy pet?

Astrid | Cycles of waking…

Do you think we're going the same way as the dogs? It's the question everybody asks yet at the same time they want to avoid the answer. One thing is that the symptoms are different, the dogs all died of spontaneous involuntary asphyxiation, everyone knows that, but nobody knows why. With us, we've been told we could wake up at any second, it's been established in the last week or so within recognised medical circles that we are supposedly choosing to sleep. The doctor doing his rounds at the hospital demonstrated that Lance is simply sleeping. He pulled Lance's eyelid up with his thumb and his pupil was missing – all I could see was the white part of his eye. The doctor told me this phenomenon was known as DeSilva's Syndrome – which is a normal reflex which takes place when a person closes their eyes. Your eye rolls outwards and upwards as the lid closes. He then said Lance and the others like him were fighting to stay asleep, as usually the pupil would be visible. The doctor smiled apologetically and finished up by saying the sleep specialists didn't know if this was an unconscious reflex or a form of active communication. That a sleeper's brainwaves show the cycles of waking and sleep one would expect to see in a healthy person, so the reasons and causes were still shrouded in intrigue.

I saw the same doctor in the canteen later and asked if I could join him, his name was Dr Charles. He talked about the many ways different cultures around the world were responding to their sleepers. Depending on where we're from we embody different culturally shaped ideas about illness. He'd done studies about how we learn our reactions to illnesses and code them into our brains, like when we experience an unfamiliar sensation, we will fit it into a set of schematics we already understand. For instance, a headache could mean an oncoming migraine to somebody who suffers from them, or alternatively it could spell an early sign of a brain tumour to someone who had a relative who had died from one. So, the pathology has a life of its own from the watcher's point of view, and how the sufferer reacts – it is all down to their past experiences and knowledge really. The brain links all kinds of symptoms together into chains that are purely in the mind based on the trigger illness and by then relating all this to our specific cultural background, we then react accordingly. I asked him what was being done to wake sleepers in other countries where the cultures didn't rely on western medicine, and he spoke about the exorcism of bad spirits via shamans in South America but just as he was going into more detail one of his colleagues came to take him away from me. He gave me his banana yoghurt.

I'm not sure if I have this right, but his way of seeing the sleepers is that they've somehow all chosen to fall asleep subconsciously because everybody else was doing it. It's like mass-hysteria, moral panic, or panic buying. I remember back when we were all about thirteen years old, we all had to get a measles vaccination and this girl called Tonya Bill began to panic. At first, she was wringing her hands, then her legs just went from under her, and she just collapsed on the floor, the teacher rushed over to her, but then two others, I don't remember who, also fell down, then another, and another all fainted. I felt it too, the panic, but I held on, it was like the reverse of ice down your spine, I felt my blood turn hot and shoot up from the base of my spine to the nape of my neck. I don't remember all that much except for that and the flush back into my lower belly. All the girls who fainted literally got back up within a few minutes and later that day, we all got inoculated in smaller groups.

I can't riddle it out. To me the sleepers are all experiencing some mystery primer making them feel the need to wait their issue out through the symptom of extreme rest. Or is it just another form of mass hysteria making itself known? And if it is, how does that explain the sleeping animals and disappearing fish? No-one is taking the animals into account, maybe the plants are asleep too. I wanted to ask Dr Charles what he thought but I knew I probably wouldn't see him again. I looked at my watch to check the time he was in the canteen, maybe he'd be back tomorrow. I tried to talk to Mum and Synnøve about all this, but I could tell they weren't following me.

Last night, I made Lance a tape of some tunes we liked and when I sat with him at the temporary hospital this afternoon, I put one of the headphone buds in his ear and the other in mine. I'd taped Flirt Reynolds's show off Red Shoes FM that was playing all this rave and house stuff he likes. I watched the room around me as we listened to this house track called Good Life by Inner City that he loves. So many families in the same boat.

Gene | My life had gathered…

I ended up spending two days in London. After that first night when I stayed at the station with Hope, I got a bus back towards Hyde Park where more people than I've ever seen together in my life had gathered at Speakers' Corner. Just like I'd seen in the papers, hundreds of tents had been pitched and there were protestors everywhere, but so many people were just sleeping on the ground, rolled up in bedding around the bases of trees and under bushes. I didn't know if they were being cared for or if they were dead from exposure like Luca was. The Hare Krishna guys were out giving people free food, and the Sikhs were further down towards Hyde Park Corner with their langar. I queued for a curry after listening to a few different speakers. Some called for storming the Houses of Parliament, others advocated taking amphetamines to stay awake and party, one was a soldier saying all war was internecine but that we should all learn martial arts, another spoke about breeding cats, another droned on about unusual lunar cycles and tide rhythms being out of balance.

The army was lining Hyde Park Place and Park Lane in their

gigantic Bedford wagons, and I could see some officers taking afternoon tea on the pavement in front of the Dorchester Hotel where all the famous actors and singers usually hole up.

I could see a massive group of men and women digging holes in the lawns across from Speakers' Corner; huge mounds of soil were everywhere. I stopped to talk to this girl who was watching these crazed moles. She told me they were doing it to stay awake. They would dig one hole and then go onto another and another. Some were using tree branches or their hands, just clawing at the mud; others had shovels and picks which was weird as I couldn't work out where they'd got them from. The girl asked me for some money, but I told her if she was hungry, she should get a curry off the Sikhs or the Buddhists. She told me she wanted it for drugs – she knew where she could score, and we could go together. When I shrugged, she stuck her middle-finger up at me and told me get fucked, before running off full-pelt in a straight line across the green in front of me. I watched her become a dot as the heavens opened. To keep dry, I headed over to a line of trees surrounded by tall bushes for cover. As soon as I got myself positioned beneath this huge plane tree, I was hit senseless by this awful, bad smell. It was like a mixture of shit, ripe berries, strong cheese, raw meat, and off-milk. I wandered around the tree to see if I could get away from the smell but it got stronger, it was then that I saw the body of a man hanging by his neck from a rope, the birds had pecked his puffed up, purple face. His feet were about three foot above the ground. I don't know how long he'd been there – I don't know about these things, but the stink was too much to think straight. I've not seen a dead body before, so I was reeling, that's when

I stumbled backwards and fell over a sleeper on the ground, but they didn't stir. The flies buzzed in the shit that had filled this guy's trousers when he lynched himself and I was sick all over myself as I discovered the extent of the carnage. I put my hand on the corpses wallet that lay discarded below his suspended feet, opened bare like a book. I didn't pick it up, I picked myself up off the floor instead and ran off into the rain, just like anyone else would.

The bad weather persisted but I made it through the crowds in the direction of Green Park and Piccadilly and up Shaftesbury Avenue into Theatreland. I ended up at this old boozer in Soho called The Blue Posts, I had to get warm and give my clothes a chance to dry out and a bit of a wash in the loos. This gay old boy came and sat next to me at the bar. He began to chat me up by saying I looked strong and asked what I was into, but I told him I wasn't like that, he said, you will be, love. I told him about the dead body in the park and he said he'd heard about mass graves being dug for all the queers who had been murdered by the police on Hampstead Heath since the riots began. He didn't look like he was lying. Things like this happen all the time around the world. Just because it's happening in England, don't for one second think this is a new thing, he said, before he put a tune on the jukebox. He didn't wait for it to play, he just pulled on his jacket and slid out the door into the street. Weirdly, it was my Dad's favourite song, Knowledge of Beauty by Dexys Midnight Runners.

The pub was on Berwick Street, so I was able to keep an eye on the shoppers going back and forth to see if I could spot Bob and Beetroot. Eventually, I went to have a browse at the long box CDs in the record shops hoping to see the two of them. But I couldn't get the dead guy in the tree out of my mind. After looking in the shop, I went back to the pub for another drink to get rid of the smell of 'suicide man' out of my nostrils. It had emptied out quite a bit, but a few people were still sitting about. I took a seat by the window and watched people come and go along the street. At the crossroads, outside the front door, a group of half-naked muscle men with painted chests running in a circle around a really big bloke dressed as a paramilitary in a balaclava with a gold crown perched on top; he was alternately blowing a whistle and barking commands at them. One of the painted men set off a flare and it created a plume of yellow smoke which engulfed them all; as the cloud rose up, I could see the men disappearing up the street running after their king. A few seconds later a seriously witchy woman with a total of two teeth in her head made me jump by slapping her flat palms on the window where I sat, I thumped the window with the side of my fist in return and she just cackled and walked off in the same direction as the painted men.

After a while, the late-night bars began to open, and I found myself in this place called The Brain Club on Wardour Street. I just hid in there all night, dancing on the floor, trying to keep going. It was almost possible to forget the chaos going on everywhere yet some businesses carried on like nothing was wrong, I saw gangs of kids looting shops, but clubs and pubs ploughed on regardless – people needed to dance I guess. There was probably fewer staff than normal, but you couldn't tell, bars like this were usually always rammed and you always had to wait for a drink and tonight wasn't that much different. The dancefloor had an NYC subway car parked in the middle of it (I wonder how they got it down there), and whilst people were boogieing in the aisle of its interior, others were sleeping, sat with their heads in their hands or on the tables where revellers would usually hang out drinking or snogging. Nobody approached or spoke to me the whole time I was in there; London can be like that sometimes. Tonight, more so maybe.

When the club closed at about two in the morning, I just walked the streets until sun-up, I walked as far as Islington High Street and then looped back around Kings Cross, Farringdon, Holborn, I walked for hours and for miles. At dawn in Kings Cross, I saw two men climbing out of a third-floor window on to a balcony carrying a fish tank, which they proceeded to throw onto the street below. Tropical fish and water smashed and splashed like a supersonic nightmare, broken glass everywhere! This was followed by people appearing at windows up and down the street trying to make out the flapping, soon-to-be dead fish on the road. In Angel, a mad man in a red cape ran past me screaming at the top of his voice, he told me to run for my life, but the street ahead of me was empty. Gray's Inn Road was blockaded by a pile of old bed frames and mattresses someone had set on fire, they'd been emptied out of a derelict sanatorium which was still on fire – I could see columns of black smoke unfurling out of the upper floor windows and out through a portion of the roof where the tiles had fallen through the rafters. Rain was lightly falling, and I could hear a quiet crackling as the flames tried to survive regardless. I didn't ring the fire brigade, I couldn't see a phone box and there was literally, nobody around.

The uncanny embodied itself in a stutter throughout the night and early morning. I'd walk for a mile without seeing anybody or hearing anything, then out of nowhere I'd witness an event so out of character with my everyday shit that I froze, hoping I wouldn't get engulfed in what I was seeing. I don't know how to say it, but sometimes I can get by by simply standing still. It's as if I'm watching television and the mentals can't see me, that they operate within their realm of mayhem without knowing I'm there; it's hard to explain but I felt like I was an observer who couldn't be touched. I was in a trance the whole time which I put down to a lack of sleep and exhaustion from walking so far, combined with the cold and all the utter weirdness I'd encountered.

Among the things I saw, there was this guy, who looked like Art Garfunkel in a stripey multi-coloured polo neck, who was crashing his car into a wall, only he was doing it at a very low speed, just gradually crushing the front of his car into the bricks. I could hear the grille buckling and front headlights crunching as his front wheels turned and I could smell burnt rubber. The tyres fraying against the metal of the wheel arch rims as they cut into them. The curly haired driver saw me but carried on, his screwed-up face turning as beetroot as Beetroot's does.

Sometime later, I smelt weed coming from a Princess parked along Southampton Row. This black kid with an eye patch wound down his window and spat on my coat, I just stopped and stared at his screwball eye, but I didn't retaliate – there were about four lads in the car, I got a sense they had all stopped what they were doing to focus on me. I thought they were going to tax me, but they just burst out laughing as the spitter sealed himself in again, rolling up the window saying, tsk just move on, man. And that was it, I didn't look back.

By The Long Water in Hyde Park, just down from the Peter Pan statue, I saw two people getting kicked on the ground by three policewomen, they were balled up on their sides, hands on heads, to protect themselves. The women had night sticks and were really going to town on their quarry. One of the coppers saw me watching and pointed her stick at me, stop where you are sir. Where are you going, sir? Get the fuck back here, sir. Sir, get over here, now… Come on, what are you waiting for, sir? And I just legged it. I saw she had all this blood running out of her mouth and down her chin, like she'd bitten her tongue or been punched in the face, I don't know. When I looked back, she was wiping her mouth on her fluorescent coat sleeve. From a distance, I continued watching as the women moved off down the path. I hid in a laurel bush for a long time in case they came back. As time went on, I got my arse in gear and shifted it across the park.

I also saw but stayed away from, two or three giant bonfires in Green Park and a dormer van ablaze down Constitution Hill. Mounted military horsemen were charging small groups of protesters across the park's lawns; they seemed to be trampling sleeping people as they went. Maybe the sleeping bags I saw were empty. One of the horsemen was blowing a bugle, another was holding a ceremonial sword aloft roaring as he went.

I found myself in a kind of daze as I walked, and ran, and walked. This trance-like state was beginning to take me over and it was mixed with a wild kind of hangover and growing hunger. Although I was confronted with these mad encounters, I couldn't intervene. I wish I was more articulate; I want to describe it better for you, the way I felt, but you'd have to have been there. And you probably know other people who were. Did they see what I did?

Nothing seemed all that weird after the first morning, maybe it was something like shellshock; the horsemen galloping across sleepers, dead people in trees, screaming women, gay muscle men setting off smoke flares, people out clubbing like it's a normal Saturday night, weed smoking shadows, tropical fish rain, infernos in the rain. I'd even forgotten to keep an eye out for Beetroot and Bob. In the back of my mind, I knew they were OK, but then again, how could I know that (I heard Nutty Snacks' voice asking me the same thing). I pictured Bob and Beetroot heading back to Ealing Broadway with carrier bags full of import 12"s but then I'd imagine them both bound and gagged in a riverside warehouse with bloodied pillowcases on their heads.

I sunk down on the steps of the Albert Memorial, and fought as best I could not to sleep, but I lay down anyway. Luckily, I awoke – a skateboarder doing tricks off the lower steps snapped me out of the murk; the midday sun eclipsed by the dome of the Albert Hall. Kensington Gardens had become fairly empty and the sky a kind of gold behind the trees. There was no way to find Beetroot and Bob now, I decided to look for a bus to bust me out of the capital.

Some fifteen minutes later after leaving my spot on the monument, when I was walking up Kensington towards Hyde Park Corner, I heard a continuous roar of voices steadily getting louder to a kind of hellish crescendo; I stopped to hear where the noise was coming from and then all of a sudden, I saw it. About a quarter of a mile up ahead of me, a crowd of, I don't know, it seemed like over a hundred running people appeared out of a side street, they were screaming and shouting as one, and they were just coming at me. I could hear the screams and shouts getting louder and louder the closer they got, it became deafening, but I was rooted to the spot, like a bunny in the headlights. I watched, paralysed – cars got trashed as these nutters ran over their roofs and jumped on their bonnets, one after the other, everything in this tangle's seething path was consumed – bicycles, bins, bus stops, parking meters. I made a break for it, I ran, I had to, and as I ran, the frontrunners in the crowd caught up and outpaced me. I saw this ginger guy running to my right and he gave me a crazed grin as he left me behind, I caught the words – I am the son of Cerberus and we are the children of the dog, as he cartwheeled past. Then I was consumed in the frenzy of galloping runners, I was in the forge of life, no choice but to act in terror, it was purer and scarier than anything I've ever felt since being born probably, in anything, even love... even love. I can't tell you how immediate and awful, yet amazing it felt all at once. Maybe it was like having your mind torn apart or having your head stuffed inside a bear's mouth. I don't have the right words for you, but that's as close to saying what it all was. It was like being eaten – the smell, the noise, the closeness of the wild inside us that we keep away from. Before I knew it, I was screaming too, arms flailing, and grabbing onto others trapped in the turbo.

The Chorus | The vertigo of the infinite…

This is the cause of your unease. The vertigo of the infinite. The ecstasy of endless possibility and the greediness of the void. The visibility and pressing consistency of the nothingness that awaits every one of us – the oppressive and pure endless lack of anything that weighs on our minds, pushing at our fragile sanity, jostling our fears.

And after the short but dense labyrinth of our time, after the human project comes to its ends, my mind falls to the forests that will reclaim everything once more, the battalions of trees by the zillion that will eventually strangle every piece of every city, every town, and farm. Everything will disappear under the boughs and branches of the never-ending verdancy that will creep/march upon our world like Birnam Wood did in Macbeth. The trees will trample all in their path in a creeping slow motion – all things human will be lost beneath root plates, vines, as well as the spreading moss, the ceaseless rains, silt, and sand. Mankind's roofs will cave in, and their brick and concrete walls will break up into the understorey. Within three hundred years you won't even be able to find all that much of us, our bones having been crushed to splinters then dust then less. Extinction is a procession of singularities, like the dinosaurs, the woolly mammoth, the Irish Elk, the dodo, the fin whale, the Syrian Wild Ass, the Elm tree, the Quagga, the robin redbreast, Przewalski's Horse, the Black Rhino, the cheetah, the Red Roman, the Hawaii chaff flower, the sabre-toothed tiger, the Franklin tree, the dogs, and like us humans, we're all taking our turn as nature moves unstoppably like a desert's dunes. It will carry on straight ahead, on this course, until the day our planet is consumed by the sun as it dies and then, in time, becomes a red giant and all we ever were will have transformed into something else entirely.

Hope | She was half certain…

At some point when he was still up in London, Gene rang me from a phone box to tell me he hadn't found Beetroot or Bob – there was no trace, he wanted to check with me to see if they'd turned up here in Eton Wick, but they hadn't.

Gene shared with me that London had been hell, he'd even seen a dead body in Hyde Park which really upset him (and me), been involved in riots, and how he had to get drunk in order to function.

After he hung up, I phoned Beetroot's mum again but all she had to say was that she was half-certain he'd turn up eventually because he always did. Was half-certain good enough?

Mum told me virtually everybody at the care home was a sleeper now, and how she thought old people seemed to succumb more easily but who knows? Dad's factory has closed properly, he's even laid off the security. He's at a loss for the right thing to do. Just leaving the factory empty is a risk, but his income has dried up and he can't go into his reserves else he won't be able to reopen after the madness ends.

Yesterday, Gene invited me to go for a walk in the fields with him. He looked different – visibly troubled by what he'd seen in London. He confessed he didn't know why the mayhem of the capital hadn't spread outwards –he thought we were maybe just days or weeks away from it flooding outwards towards Eton Wick.

Gene depicted these weird pockets of normality in the middle of London, that the lunacy had been confined to large public spaces in the main, but each individual location had somehow attracted a different faction which somehow dictated the wider mood of the crowd. He said he felt like he was driving in a storm, steaming on through despite bad visibility, that he was in a trance and it seemed as if everything was happening to someone else. For someone who mostly grunts and sneers, he painted a very vivid picture. I'm seeing a very different side to him.

Gene told me about how he saw people drinking from puddles, people looting a massive Rumbelows whereas Foyles Books next door remained untouched, about a discarded Chinese flower dragon that came alive in the wind, about army horses trampling sleeping bodies, and he showed me a notepad he'd filled up on the train with a list of some of the conspiracy theories he'd heard at Speakers' Corner – he tore out the page of scribbled words and said he didn't want it anymore but it was the closest thing he had to a witness.

Gene was obviously still worried about Beetroot and Bob and I could see it weighing on him. I asked him about Rowan, whether he'd seen her or still loved her which just came out and sounded utterly unrelated to anything. He told me quite stiffly that Rowan didn't matter anymore. I thanked him for walking me home and assured him that everything was going to be OK but my words sounded hollow; I don't think Gene was really there. I went to hug and kiss him on the cheek, but he dodged me, almost like he was flinching, and then he gave me a look, as I tried to keep my balance on the doorstep.

After Gene left, I went up to my room and got in bed and worried about London and wondered when we'd all be digging holes and setting each other on fire.

The next evening, I holed up in The Fawn in Windsor with Rowan who was out with some of her mates from Daniels. I wanted to tell her Beetroot was missing, but at first, I just let her talk, but she didn't have a lot to say except that working in the toy department was alright, she'd been hard at work on her art and whenever I had a free afternoon we should go and look at what she'd been up to. She said Simon P had invited us all to this free party in Slough, and did I want to go? She wasn't sure where it was but had a good idea where it might be. She asked me to invite Astrid too, but I said it would be a waste of time because she was looking in on Lance most of the time, and she wouldn't want to party in a million years. When I told her about Beetroot, she looked concerned, but I could tell her mind was on other things. Also, I'd tried not to mention Gene, but in the end, I told her what he'd seen up in London, that he'd tried to find Beetroot and Bob. Unexpectedly, she began to cry, so I gave her a hug, she just folded into my arms and sobbed, she couldn't get her words out. We stepped outside the pub for some air in the end because her work buds were all looking at her whilst trying not to notice at the same time; being boys, they didn't do anything but watch her like a bunch of goldfish. Rowan wanted to know when it was all going to end, she was terrified of what was coming. I calmed her down by saying there was nothing to be afraid of, we were in Eton Wick and not Hyde Park, I was really repeating what Gene had said to put me at ease. Again, I felt like I was lying to myself, that the mayhem and havoc were lying in wait for me – for us, and that nothing could stop it.

When we went back inside the pub, this techicoloured nightmare called Brendan O'Hagan-Denny had installed himself at the head of our table. Dressed up in a pinstripe shirt, braces and a dicky bow he'd found in the RSPCA shop, he was like a cross between Beeker out of The Muppets, Garfield, and Robin Day off Question Time (without the wit). Everything he said was a flat joke only he could see the funny side of – he'd laugh at his own voice and deliberations harder and for longer than everybody else – always gobbing off at the top of his stupid toff accent, sucking on cigarettes as if they were ice lollies. I generally walk the other way when I see him coming but tonight, he was sitting with Rowan's friends. He was mainly poking fun at the futility of setting a car bomb off to destroy a castle which had stood unblemished for about a thousand years and now there was a flimsy metal curtain erected around the outside of the wall, as if that could protect it from a second incident. He laboured on about it being the IRA as it has been a few weeks since the London Stock Exchange bombing and about the fact there were no casualties. He didn't register how bored our faces were looking, he didn't even notice four people leave the table to go and stand at the bar and gradually all the others went out into the garden to talk amongst themselves. He concluded his broadcast by announcing that many of the shops and pubs in Peascod Street, the High Street, and the cobbled streets had been boarded up including The Trout, and some sentry boxes for checkpoints had been built at certain points around the castle and along the river. Stuff most of us already knew. Once Rowan and I left, he was sitting at our very large table all by himself.

Anyway, fuck Brendan, all that's really occupying me is Beetroot and Gene, and how I upset Rowan so easily. I think, in fact, I know Beetroot's gone. I don't feel like he's a sleeper though, he's either on the grift, running with a pack, or he's just fled off like I always suspected he would, but then I'm forgetting how scared he was acting when the riot broke out, how panicked he became. Yet as I got drunker, I began to concoct ways out for him. I entertained the fact he may just prefer his friends to me, that I was just some test he had to pass, some box he had to tick; I was Hope, the first girlfriend kit. I'm seventeen, he's nineteen, it fits, we lost our virginity to one another. He was important to me and more than alright, but then again, I just can't get a clear picture of him in my future – he's shimmering like a ghost on the horizon; why was I absolving myself of worry? With every pint I burrowed my head further into the sand. Gene thought that Beetroot had become a sleeper, so maybe I have to feel the same way Astrid does about Lance, her patient vigil, full of hope, like my name – but I feel next to nothing. I am both numb and bloated.

Après pub, I went home and fell on my bed; the bedroom ceiling was spinning, so I got up out of bed again and was sick all over the floor. I had Every Rose Has Its Thorn by Poison in my head because the girls at the pub kept on playing it on the jukebox.

It's an awful song to have stuck in your head when the room is flying around at ninety-five hundred miles an hour.

A few hours later, I awoke again to darkness. I needed air so I hung myself out the bedroom window. There was a strong summer wind blowing in from the river which was pressing my hair into my face, I pushed it away and tried to focus on the hazy distant lights up on the relief way, but I fell back inside the room and vomited again. This time I was sick in torrents all over the sketch I made of Luca last year, the one that kept on peeling off the wall. I ran for the light switch and saw that in my drunken haze I had torn up my tattoo designs of Cerberus too. I had no memory of its obliteration.

The tatters of the sketch pad were all around my feet and on my bed; some pages had vomit on them, and the room stank; I lit an incense stick but the sweet smell made it all a lot worse and I vomited again – this time out the window.

A whole summer's worth of careful and precise illustration, all gone; my ideas so fresh but not yet memorised, fucking well lost. I sat down amidst the ripped, the ruined sheets of my sketch book and tore them into long strips then I staggered to my feet and went to the open window with them. One by one, I set fire to the pieces with a fag lighter and let them go. I watched them sail on the wind, drifting downwards into the garden like flaming birds. After sending a dozen or so slithers out into the night air, I set fire to the remainder of pile. I was mesmerised as the flames began to lick upwards, fanned by the breeze; that was when I shoved everything off the window ledge. Within seconds, the burning sketchbook and my drawings were flaming up into a black ball on the patio far below. Then I burnt Luca, I watched his smiling form as it was annihilated by small and swift blue flames; his right arm went first, then his white vest, his contoured neck, his toned chest and lower torso, then his handsome face from right to left. I wondered if the real Luca burnt in the same order.

After Luca's portrait was destroyed, I blew the ashy remains away into the air just to see them rain down like orange-black filoplumes. As my eyes grew accustomed to the dark, I could see I wasn't alone; someone in the garden backing onto ours was watching me through their open French doors. I shouted that there was nothing to worry about, the fire is out. They didn't move. The featureless human shape just watched me, silhouetted by a weak yellow light that glowed from somewhere deep inside their house; the ember ball of their cigarette pulsed as it slowly travelled up and down an invisible dark track that linked their left hip to their mouth.

Rowan | Their mad bones...

When I got home after work last night, I found Mum sorting through dog bones on the living room carpet. She told me they'd gotten muddled up when the box she had put them in slid off the back seat of the car; she could no longer tell which bones were Trudy's and which were Griff's or Meg's.

All Mum would say is that she wanted her dogs back with her forever and they wanted to be with her in return. They're all here with their mummy now, she told me.

I watched her running her hand over their phantom fur-lined bodies, inches above their mad bones, as if she were stroking their backs. I noticed A Room with a View was playing on the TV at top volume – Denholm Elliott was busy laughing at angels painted on the ceiling of the Basilica; I made an involuntary wail as I watched my mum in this alien state, lost to all things except her dog relics.

They haven't gone. They're here with me, aren't you my little loves, she said. Her words battled for clarity and understanding versus the strong smell in the room, the mould, moss and earth.

I don't think I'll ever be able to get the scene out of my head,

Mum's canine reliquary; the three skulls of her old dogs sitting on a cushion each like the Crown Jewels – Mum cross-legged on the floor amongst them, covered head-to-toe in mud. When she told me to put the kettle on, I just turned on my heels and left the room with the full intention of leaving the house; I looked over my shoulder to glimpse her holding Trudy's skull out to me in her outstretched palms. She said my name once, Rowan, before I closed the living room door on her. Everything inside me screamed 'run'. I grabbed my art bag from by the front door and left the house as quickly as I could.

And then I couldn't stop crying. As I ran, I could feel the tears on my face fly off – the spray cans and work lamp inside my bag bruising my left hip as they bounced around. When I ran out of breath, I stopped and sat on the curb. Then I got up and I ran again. I repeated this a few times until I eventually neared the railway viaduct. But I couldn't clear my mind, it screeched and spun like a chafing zoetrope.

Hope had scared me tonight at the pub when she told me Beetroot and Bob had vanished on their trip to London, and of the nightmarish things Gene had seen. I felt like I couldn't breathe, my skin was hot, and I needed cool air. Bonkers images in my head conjured themselves involuntarily; visions that reared up into view every few seconds. I saw a mushroom cloud bursting out of Windsor Castle's Round Tower, Gene's head in a noose – fingers clawing at the rope, a raging inferno at a rave – hundreds of people on fire streaming into the fields, a man tumbling through a clear blue sky in white robes, an angry black-eyed, red-skinned pig screeching. And then I saw the dogs' skeletons re-assembling themselves like they were on a stop-motion animated show for kids. All the while Trudy's boney dog tail could be seen wagging back and forth like a metronome – tick tack, tick tack.

When I finally got to The Brocas on the north bank of the Thames, I found a place to sit and dangle my feet in the water – I didn't think to take my pumps off.

From where I was sitting, I could see a large army lorry parked outside the boarded-up Trout on the other side of the river – soldiers were jumping down from the back of it then forming into ranks along the pavement – only the bark of their squad leader could be heard – the men and women were all moving in silence. They each had a gun and body armour on. I watched as the soldiers waited and waited; after ten minutes or so a second, identical lorry rounded the bend from Alexandra Gardens and soon the statue-like waiting soldiers had all climbed inside it and were gone into the night. Maybe they were heading for London, or the M25 wall – I don't know. The first lorry sat empty, perhaps it had broken down. Windsor looked still except for the blinking orange zebra lights at the crossing. The pulsing streetlight and the cold water surface of the Thames – the only sound and movement.

Astrid | Only happens in stories…

I have signed up to train as a nurse. I can't help anybody stood at the check-out in a motorway newsagent. I join up next week and will be training at the old hospital in Windsor.

I tend to see Lance most days even though I know he's in good care. I wonder if it's karma, his becoming a sleeper, because I kissed Enos – but I know that's the kind of thing which only happens in stories, yet I can't shake the uncomfortable feeling it's all connected. I confided in Synnøve, but she told me it's a storyteller's burden to see patterns everywhere – to connect disparate things together – also to naturally put themselves at the centre of the universe – she mentioned Aristotle, but I couldn't follow her, but I will.

I think coincidences only occur because the levels of chance are mathematical – with the finite proportions of actions in the universe at any one time, there's a good chance you will witness a fleeting feeling of synergy here and there. But maybe that's a writer's lot perhaps; I mean, why do I read? I suppose I read to understand my surroundings better, and we probably adapt so we can interpret and apply metaphors, portents, analogies like a second tongue. We read so we can unlock our future by seeing how those who went before us managed. Yet there'll always be some of us who will forever confuse literature with life; supposedly, I'll always be on the lookout for a pattern when what I really want to do is see what lies in wait round the next bend. I think I do it to predict the future. But I still carry on in the hope this will put that kind of anxiety at bay. Like the writer Paul Bowles said, life all seems limitless but it's not.

No amount of thinking about it will bring Lance back to me though. I want him and I need him. This is my strength, my core, I know what needs to happen now. After all, without love, our lives remain concealed and that's no way to be.

Gene | Raging fire

I dreamt I saw a raging fire…

Slave | Lo Cerberus...

Quickly, it all became dark as if the sun had suddenly been dropped by the sky. I wish I didn't have to make the journey to the pit. I wanted to be there already. My feet were still wet and cold from dangling them in the river and they showed no sign of drying out.

There was nobody, not a soul out on the path back to Slough that runs parallel to the railway viaduct – the M4 seemed bereft of cars / I saw a fox that stopped in my path to stand and watch me approach through the quiet night / At the Common Lane bridge I laboured up the steps onto the viaduct – the diesel trains don't run this late / Soon, I was at The Pit – I walk quickly when I'm cold – don't we all? / I struggled in through the break in the chain link fence when I reached yard of buses and trucks / My bag caught on some barbwire – ripping a hole about the size of a ten pence piece in the fabric / I weaved my way through the maze of dead buses by following the coloured arrows I'd spray painted last winter / I stopped and checked out my recent piece – the dashing dog with Auden's rabbit quote (I remember seeing Gene and Bob the day I created it. I watched them wandering around in the gloom before

I ran like the years – my paint still dripping) / I veered around the bottomless mechanic's pits / I swung my light towards the blue double doors / I was whispering the words, As Above, So Below, as I dashed down the stairs like their sacrament protected me from the waiting blackness / I arrived at the foot of the stairs, the dark lip of the bowl ahead, dead bang / Beyond it I could see my newest (partially finished) fresco / Then the sound came in / A distant dog sounded off in the night :: One bark :: Two barks together – a string of five bursts – but it was all in my head / I obeyed my need to answer the phantom dog's call / My chorus circled into the bowl / I could hear it thin out through the hollows.

It's funny – I often think that I am working in silence, but the water never relents dripping/running as it moves through its mysterious city of pipes and tunnels.

The smells and sounds send my thoughts back towards Mum, her skeletal pets, her dominating madness made of endings and fear. The moss and mould in the living room carpet (the living tomb), the dogs' grey, gnarled teeth, the endless black of their eye cavities. I can't cure her; I don't make a difference to her – I can't bring the dogs back. With the bones she is exactly where she's wanted to be for the last fifteen years. Not with me but with her pets; their ghosts and her memories of them aren't enough. Could she not sense that there's nothing there, there's no trace of their souls – it's just bones – dust, splinters, earth matter. She can't even tell which bone is from which dog. She can't tell that even, and that should matter.

2. Six eyes can wait...

The creation of the demon dog's six eyes can wait. Every time I spray paint one of my dog murals, I render the eyes last of all. I feel compelled to replace all those wallpaper dogs' eyes I'd scratched out when I was a little girl. An eye for an eye.

It will take all night to finish this fresco then I can consider going home to help Mum, finding professional help for her, I need to try and limit the fallout at the necropolis – the disturbance of the graves won't go unnoticed, she'll lose her position – that's inevitable. I must clean out the house – release its locked-up ghosts once and for all – I have to talk to Gene - he's never out of my head. I absolutely need to get my life in order before it all falls away.

Down beneath the beast's dripping feet, I spray paint my alias then just two words, Lo Cerberus.

Astrid | It's gonna be alright...

Synnøve came and got me from the hospital at the end of my shift – I rushed to kiss Lance on his sleeping lips – he has no scent now except the sterile wipe us nurses use to clean the sleepers' surfaces down. He looks dead. If only I could discover whether the forces of cause and effect are within my power. Can I compel the stars to revolve around him and reverse all our fortunes? My thoughts are nearly as heavy as feelings – I see that rather than understand the problem of the sleepers, the only thing my presence in the hospital serves to demonstrate is my irrelevance and the elimination of all finality.

Sweat chills my body in private as I wait in the car park for Synnøve. My sister gives me a miniature of vodka after I've done my seatbelt up. We go home to get dressed up - a party, one last shot at voluntary annihilation. I took half an 'e' and felt the pixelated rise and bristling rush amongst the skin cells. I'd be coming up as soon as we arrived at The Pit, Synnøve told me. You'll love it, she said. It will help you remember the night, the very juice of it, as she swallowed the other half.

2. I saw hope...

Out in the dancing, strobe-lit crowd, the fluttering light beams synched to the thump of the DJ's beats; I saw Hope, I saw Rowan, Gene was there. Amid two hundred and fifty souls following a pulse, we congregated, moved in rhythm, smiled at one another, embraced, hung on to one another like we were in a raging ocean, it felt like we were all in love; and we followed the music through the night towards an implication of an ending we feared yet still couldn't see. We just danced on and on for the times we can't remember and danced for the people we can't forget; our sleepers, our dear Luca... We toasted the spray paint frescos of Rowan – the three gigantic heads of Cerberus watched us from behind the decks.

We strained to feel the earth through the soles of our Adidas, Puma, Pro-Keds and Green Flash clad feet, we were concrete dancefloor fabulists like the girl in Hans Christian Andersen's the Red Shoes. We couldn't stop dancing even if wanted to.

The pounding 909s conjured an amplified mimic of a dog's thumping tail on the carpet until they paused for a few moments. Slow synth washes and basslines began to gain precedence, commanding us all to raise our hands above our heads and reach into the surf of blinding searchlights that were feeling their way out for us from the stage. All over again, the recursive percussion started to fade in and there it was, in the glare, we saw one another underlined, ardent smiles on our mouths. All we wanted was for everything to be alright, we hoped it would be, and the music played forever.

Epilogue

The Chorus | What you are…

The heavy-set Alsatian is stood close to the centre of a conifer-encircled frozen lake. It is barking; you can see miniature clouds of breath, yet you cannot hear its call.

You are aware that it is bracingly cold, and you shiver as you stand at the lake's edge; then you gradually become aware of more dogs. As if obeying some far-off command or design; crowds of animals begin to engulf the surface of the lake en masse, surging in from the line of tree cover. The ice becomes obscured by the rivers of dogs. Their amassing bodies transforming the lake's silver surface into a writhing seethe of brown, black, white, orange, and golden fur.

These magnificent, much-loved beasts of earth and stone, woodland valley and mountain pass.

Lo Cerberus.

Acknowledgements

I continue to write to honour the memory of my beloved Mum, Jackie Roberts, who died in 2019. I wish you were still here with us all. I'll never run out of tears. I dedicate all my books to my family and good friends.

Thanks and gratitude to my family and friends especially Rose, Matt Usher, Hanna Lambert, Steve Taylor, Jon Woolcott, Mark McDonald, Richard Jones, Steve Nash & The Berkshire Blaggers, Colette Roberts, Alan Roberts sr, Hannah Jury, AM Haywood, Trudi Clarke, Sandy Fish, Walter Henry's Bookshop (Bideford), and everybody who buys, reviews and reads my stories - they are for you.

I miss, honour and remember family members: Mum, Eva Beamer, Elaine Roberts, Madge Carlisle, Douglas Ashley, Elizabeth Parr, Eva Pugh, Bernard Roberts, and Peter Roberts. To my late friend, Roger Balfour (1966-2022).

The many songs of Cerberus

Boris Gardiner - I Want To Wake Up With You (Revue 1986)
Womack & Womack - Teardrops (4th & Broadway 1988)
Eddy Arnold - The Cattle Call (EMI 1955)
11:59 - T-Minus-60 (Ticking Time 1990)
Levi 167 - Something Fresh To Swing To (B-Boy 1987)
Boogie Down Productions - Why Is That? (Jive 1989)
Guy - Her (Uptown / MCA 1991)
Mantronix (feat. Wondress) - Got To Have Your Love (Capitol 1989)
Johnny Nash - There Are More Questions Than Answers (CBS 1972)
Inner City - Good Life (Virgin 1988)
Eddy Grant - Electric Avenue (Ice 1983)

Funkadelic - Maggot Brain (Westbound 1971)
Bruce Springsteen - Tougher Than The Rest (CBS 1987)
Ten City - That's The Way Love Is (Atlantic 1988)
Eric B & Rakim - Seven Minutes of Madness Remix of Paid in Full (4th & Broadway 1987)
Beats International - Dub Be Good To Me (Go! Beat 1990)
The SOS Band - Just Be Good To Me (Tabu 1983)
Three Dog Night - Joy To The World (Probe 1970)
JS Bach - Adagio BWV 974
Curtis Mayfield & Ice T - Return of Superfly (Capitol 1990)
Curtis Mayfield - We Are The People Who Are Darker Than Blue (Curtom 1970)
NWA - Gangsta, Gangsta (Ruthless / Priority 1988)
Schoolly D - Mr Big Dick (Jive / RCA 1988)
Mantronix - King of the Beats (Capitol 1988)
T Coy - Carino (Deconstruction 1987)
The Dubliners - Lord of Dance (Polydor 1978)
Mike Dunn - Life Goes On (Westbrook 1988)
Fast Eddie - Acid Thunder (DJ International 1988)
Cutmaster DC - Brooklyn Rocks The Best (Zakia 1986)
Boys Next Door - Imperial Scratch (New Image 1986)
David Bowie - Let's Dance (EMI 1985)
Bou Khan - It's Magic (Quark 1988)
Tony G - Tony's Song (Mic-Mac 1988)
Electra - Jibaro (FFRR / London 1988)
Dynamix II (feat. Too Tough Tee) - Give The DJ a Break (Bass Station 1987)
Ice T - You Played Yourself (Sire / Warner Bros 1989)
Sweet Tee - It's Like That Y'all (Profile 1988)
Shut Up and Dance - Lamborghini - remix (Shut Up and Dance 1990)

LL Cool J - Jinglin' Baby - remix (Def Jam / CBS 1990)
Heavy D & The Boyz - We Got Our Own Thang (Uptown / MCA 1989)
Hijack - The Badman is Robbin' (Rhyme Syndicate / Epic 1989)
Think Tank - A Knife and a Fork (Hakatak / Tommy Boy 1990)
Big Daddy Kane - Young Gifted and Black (Cold Chillin' / Warner Bros 1989)
Lord Alibaski - Top Gun (Tuff City 1989)
Grandmaster Flash - Girls Love The Way He Spins (Elektra / Asylum 1985)
Mantronix - Listen to the Bass of Get Stupid Fresh part 2 (Fresh / Sleeping Bag 1986)
Man Parrish - Boogie Down Bronx (Sugar Scoop 1984)
Caron Wheeler - Livin' In The Light - Brixton Bass mix (EMI 1990)
Massive Attack - Daydreaming (Wild Bunch 1990)
En Vogue - Hold On (Atlantic 1990)
Audio Two - On the Road Again (First Priority / Atlantic 1990)
Three Times Dope - Mr Sandman (Arista 1990)
James Brown - My Thang (Polydor 1974)
JVC FORCE - Smooth and Mellow (Idlers 1990)
Melba Moore - Make Me Believe In You (Buddah 1979)
Joyce Sims - All and All - UK remix (Sleeping Bag 1988)
The Knights of The Turntables - Techno Scratch (JDC 1984)
Today - I Got the Feeling (Motown 1990)
Teddy Riley feat. Guy - My Fantasy (Motown 1989)
MC Shan - Juice Crew Law (Cold Chillin' / Warner Bros 1988)
Aleem feat. Leroy Burgess - Release Yourself - dub (Nia 1984)
World Class Wreckin' Cru - Surgery (Kru Cut / Macola 1984)
Sir Ibu of Divine Force - The Peacemaker (4th & Broadway 1989)
Def Jef feat. Etta James - Droppin' Rhymes on Drums (Delicious Vinyl / Island 1989)

The DOC - The DOC & The Doctor (Ruthless / Atlantic 1990)
Just Ice - Back to The Old School (Fresh / Sleeping Bag 1986)
Deee-lite - Groove is in the Heart (Elektra 1990)
New Order - Shellshock (Factory 1986)
The Smiths - Big Mouth Strikes Again (Rough Trade 1988)
Miracle Legion - All For The Best (Rough Trade 1987)
Run DMC - You Talk Too Much (Profile 1985)
Master Ace & Action3 - I Got Ta (Cold Chillin' / Reprise 1990)
Tyree - Acid Over (Underground 1987)
2 Puerto Ricans, A Black Man & A Dominican - Do It Properly (Grooveline 1987)
Chad Jackson - Hear the Drummer Get Wicked (Wave 1989)
Pet Shop Boys - I Want a Dog (Parlophone 1988)
Isaac Hayes - Joy (Stax 1973)
Idris Muhammad - Loran's Dance (Kudu 1974)
Doug Carn aka Abdul Rahim Ibrahim - Suratal Ihklas (Tablighi 1977)
James Brown - The Big Payback (King / Polydor 1973)
King Tee & Mixmaster Spade - Ya Better Bring a Gun (Techno Hop 1987)
DJ Jazzy Jeff & The Fresh Prince - Brand New Funk (Jive / RCA 1988)
Lakim Shabazz - All True and Living (Tuff City 1989)
Mellow Man Ace - Hip Hop Creature (Capitol 1989)
Ultimate Force - I'm Not Playing (Strong City / Uni 1989)
Trouble Funk - Drop The Bomb (Jamtu 1982)
Greg Allman - Holding On - movie version (Virgin 1989)
Chubb Rock & Howie Tee - Caught Up - remix (Select 1989)
The KLF presents The JAMS - Whitney Houston Joins The JAMs (KLF Comms 1987)
Charles B & Adonis - Lack of Love (Desire 1988)

Turntable Orchestra - You're Gonna Miss Me (Music Village 1988)
Beloved - The Sun Rising (WEA 1989)
The Aloof - Never Get Out The Boat (white label 1990)
Raze - Break 4 Love (Grove St. 1988)
Kool & The Gang - Fresh (De-Lite 1984)
808 State - Cubik (ZZTT / Tommy Boy 1990)
Salt-n-Pepa - Push It (Next Plateau 1987)
Joe Cuba - El Pito (Tico 1975)
Frankie Knuckles presents Satoshie Tomiie - Tears (FFRR 1989)
Vicious Base feat. DJ Magic Mike - Drop The Bass II
(Cheetah 1990)
Unique 3 - Weight of the Bass - 3 Ton Mix (10 1990)
Newcleus - Automan (Sunnyview 1984)
Berlin - Take My Breath Away (CBS 1986)
New Edition - Pass the Beat (Streetwise 1983)
George Clinton - Atomic Dog (Capitol 1983)
Zapp - More Bounce to The Ounce (Warner Bros 1980)
The Headhunters - God Made Me Funky (CBS 1973)
Juggy - Oily (Sue 1969)
Xavier Cugat - Perfidia (Mercury 1964)
Egyptian Lover - My House on The Nile (Egyptian Empire 1984)
Richie Rich - Salsa House (Gee Street 1989)
Rockmaster Scott & The Dynamic Three - The Roof Is On Fire - 85' remix
(Reality 1985)
Ten City - Right Back to You (Atlantic 1988)
Megadeth - Holy Wars (Capitol 1990)
Happy Mondays - Hallelujah (Factory 1990)
Ten City - Devotion (Atlantic 1988)
The Wonder Stuff - It's Yer Money I'm After Baby (Polydor 1988)
The Sugarcubes - Eat The Menu (One Little Indian 1989)

The Stone Roses - This Is The One (Silvertone 1988)
Kariya - Let Me Love You For Tonight (Sleeping Bag 1989)
Caveman - Victory (Profile 1990)
The Todd Terry Project - Weekend (Sleeping Bag 1989)
Full Force - Ain't My Type of Hype (CBS 1989)
Fishbone - Freddie's Dead (Columbia 1988)
Silver Bullet - 20 Seconds to Comply (Tam-Tam 1989)
The 45 King (feat. Lakim Shabazz) - The Red, The Black, The Green (Tuff City 1989)
Smith & Mighty (feat. Jackie Jackson) - Anyone (Three Stripe 1988)
Slayer - South of Heaven (Def Jam 1987)
Dexys Midnight Runners - Knowledge of Beauty (Mercury 1985)
Kiri Te Kanawa - O Mio Babbino Caro (Decca 1984)
Sterling Void & Paris Brightledge - It's Alright (DJ International 1987)

The publisher acknowledges Dr. Rue, The Gypsy Wave Banner as the writers of Teardrops of Womack and Womack / H Axton as the writer of Three Dog Night's Joy to the World / Mac Davis as the writer of Boris Gardiner's I Want To Wake Up With You, with full observation of Fair Usage https://www.gov.uk/guidance/exceptions-to-copyright#fair-dealing and https://www.bl.uk/business-and-ip-centre/articles/fair-dealing-copyright-explained

100% of these tunes are available on vinyl and on YouTube. I'd estimate that 65 to 75% of them are available on popular streaming platforms. In lieu of me 'busting you a tape', enjoy this track listing - it will add a pleasurable and extra dimension as well as several extra points of context within Cerberus. Thanks to all the above artists and many more for creating the soundtrack to my youth (and way beyond).